DEC 0 5 2011

Falling for Henry

1
The wish

Kate Allen plodded down the grassy hill at Greenwich Park. She and twenty other students were bound for the museum, descending through gray drizzle toward the white stone arches that marked the front entrance of London's Royal Naval College. In Fenwick's history class, they'd learned that the Naval College, built on the site of a former Tudor palace, housed a number of sixteenth-century relics. Useless, thought Kate. All useless.

"This whole trip is a waste of time," she muttered, pushing the hair away from her damp neck. She contemplated the rest of the day, how the teacher would herd them all into some kind of old-fashioned elevator and then lead the final trek home through the walking tunnel under the Thames River. Her heart thudded uncomfortably. Elevators and tunnels were on her list of things to avoid. The thought of small enclosed spaces caused a tight feeling in Kate's chest, and she fought against the old claustrophobic fear, struggling to catch her breath.

How will I ever make myself go through that tunnel? she thought, miserably. *I'll have a panic attack and everyone will think I'm a loser.* "Or ... more of a loser," she muttered, honest with herself about her profile here at this new school. Then she made a snap decision. She wouldn't go into the museum with the rest of the class. She'd go off and have a look at the walking tunnel by herself. She could try out the elevator and then gradually get used to the tunnel, so that when she had to go there with the group, she wouldn't embarrass herself. She tilted her face skyward, noticing that the rain had stopped. A good omen, she thought, as the sun came out and the tightness in her chest melted away.

As Kate bent down, pretending to tie her shoe, her auburn hair fell forward over her face. Shiny and shoulder-length, this hair was one of the few things she was proud of. She knew she wasn't beautiful, although she wished she were. She made a point of never looking at fashion magazines where all those skinny models inspired an unsettling self-consciousness about what Willow called "a full figure." Her height—only five foot two—made it hard to carry the few extra pounds she'd added since summer. How she could be gaining weight was a mystery, as her sister's cooking was terrible, and the meals they had in their tiny student apartment were nothing like what Dad used to make. Gran, whom they saw in Brighton every week or two, was a fabulous cook. Perhaps it was at Gran's where she was gaining the extra pounds. All that clotted cream and jam. Instantly, Kate felt hungry, but she pushed away thoughts of food, concentrating instead on the task at hand.

Kate finished with one shoe and began on the other. Anything to buy some time so that the other students would be well ahead when she took her little detour. She stood up carefully, trying to look nonchalant, and then smoothed down the uniform: navy jacket, navy sweater, white blouse, gray wool skirt. In all these layers she felt egg-shaped.

"Girl Humpty Dumpty rests on the hill," she muttered, warily eyeing her classmates as they passed. "Avoids walls. Stays as close to the ground as possible."

Of course, Willow would have looked gorgeous in the uniform. Her sister looked good in anything. Born to be an actress, Kate often thought jealously, knowing that she herself would never dare to think about a future with RADA, the Royal Academy of Dramatic Arts. Not that Kate cared about acting. Willow sometimes demanded that she help her with lines, and reading those scripts aloud was boring, boring, boring. This new play—Shakespeare's *Henry VIII*—was the most tedious of all, and Willow's speeches were long and difficult.

Kate's passion was numbers, mathematical problems where, once you derived the formula, everything fell into place. She wished life was that way, an equation that could be balanced, but in life there were always problems—variables you couldn't control. And life these days seemed especially off balance, making her feel as if something inside, the very shell of her being, had been cracked beyond repair.

Humpty Dumpty sat on the wall, Humpty Dumpty had a great fall, she chanted inside her head as she rested one shoe on the low iron railing that bordered the lawn at the bottom of the hill. With satisfaction, she saw Fenwick walking into the building. "Miss Fenwick," they were supposed to call her, although behind her back, the "Miss" was easily dropped. It didn't suit her. "Fenwick" was much more representative of the history teacher's pale cropped hair and the long, swift strides that reminded Kate of a greyhound. Relief washed over her that this time she had escaped notice. As she awkwardly clambered over the railing and away from the rest of the group, she darted a look behind to make sure none of her classmates was following. One of the other students, who had separated back from the others, a girl with the unfortunate name of Amandella Hingenbottom, was gazing in her direction.

"Do you 'ave a tissue?" Amandella called in the plummy accent favored by most of the kids at school. Her nose sounded plugged, Kate noted with irritation. People were always sick in London. It must be the dirty air. She shook her head firmly in response to Amandella's question, then turned away. A few moments later, she saw Amandella charging toward their disappearing classmates, becoming the last of the group to enter the large white archways of the College. The last of the group, thought Kate, except for me.

Kate hurried along the walk, ducked around the corner of the building, then leaned against its shadowed wall, panting a little and itchy in her bulky clothes. The sun was out again and the air was like a sauna. She took a deep breath. If she timed it right, she could finish her task and then catch up with the class before the teacher realized she had disappeared.

What would it be like to really disappear? she wondered. *To vanish without a trace, and never come back ...* Perhaps no one would notice that, either. It wasn't as if she had any particular friends in London. Or anywhere, she thought, pulling the watch out of her jacket pocket and estimating the time she'd need to get to the footpath and back.

She returned the watch to her pocket. Against her bare skin, watches never kept the correct hour. She'd learned this from experience. Her father had always teased her about being magnetic, but with a twinkle in his eye, she knew he'd meant charming. *Her father*. She felt heavy, missing him, somehow in slow motion, released from the laws of time and space. Lost for a few minutes, she pressed her cheek into the coolness of the shadowed wall and wished again that she could just disappear. *Without a single trace,* she mused.

Then a bell rang out at the top of the hill, marking one o'clock, and Kate came sharply back to reality, hot in the stodgy school uniform. Her father was dead and it wouldn't help to dwell on the accident. Quickly, she removed the jacket and threw it on the grass. Relieved at the resulting change in body temperature, she glanced at the scar on her hand—an odd habit that was somehow reassuring—and decided to carry on.

Later, she'd retrieve her jacket. Glancing around to make sure she was not observed, she hurried along the side of the building and then started down toward the waterfront. This, she thought, remembering the teacher's instructions, was the way to the footpath under the Thames River.

2
The tunnel

As Kate tramped across the lawn of Greenwich Park, her feet left prints on the damp grass, its limp blades flattened under her oxford shoes. She could have asked Amandella to join her; the other girl never looked very comfortable in the group, and likely she, too, would have enjoyed escape. But who needed company? Not Kate; she was hard as a boiled egg, and better off alone. Would it have been any different if she were still in New York? She thought not. Kicking repeatedly at a lump of turf, she fleetingly wished she'd had friends in New York with whom she'd kept in touch, but somehow it hadn't worked out that way. What was the point? She'd never see any of them again. Since Dad died last spring, she could vanish from the face of the earth and probably no one would care. *I could try harder*, she thought, sending the grass clump flying. Then, just as quickly, she muttered, "Why bother?"

She knew her classmates—most of them a year younger

than she, even though they were all in Year Ten together—called her stuck up. She'd heard their nickname for her—Big Apple—and tried not to think about it. Being from New York had its disadvantages. Her cheeks burned as she scratched at her waist. Why did school uniforms have to be so hot? And ugly! Dad wouldn't have made her go to this stupid school and wear these stupid clothes. He'd have known right away that she wasn't happy here, and listened when she told him how awful everything was. Unlike Willow. Not that Kate had ever really told her sister much. Why should Willow care?

She gave the lump of grass one last kick backwards onto the lawn and then doggedly turned along the Thames. The water's silver surface was deceptively smooth, making her wonder about its hidden depths. She'd heard of currents in the river, undertows that would drag you down. The very thought made her take a deep breath, filling her lungs to capacity, and then shaking her head at the dizzy feeling that accompanied too much air. Of course, the air here was polluted. Probably breathing it too deeply wasn't even healthy. Once she'd rubbed a spot on the wall in the living room she shared with Willow, and was surprised by the circle that emerged on the oily surface.

"If you're going to mess with the wall, you should get a rag and do the job properly," said Willow in a voice that always seemed too loud, too demanding.

"I'm not washing walls," retorted Kate, and quickly turned

the spot into a question mark.

"What a princess," said Willow, rolling her eyes.

Stopping for a moment at the place where the *Cutty Sark* was moored on dry land, Kate thought about how useless it was to keep a ship that couldn't float. Fenwick had told them that this was the last clipper ship ever used as a merchant vessel. She threw it a cursory look where it rested in the dirt. Nothing about history interested her. What's past is past, she thought. As she walked by the ship, the smiling witch on the figurehead momentarily caught her eye and then—or maybe it was a trick of light—its smile was replaced by a look of serious contemplation.

There were remnants of construction along the wooden walkway, and Kate had to plan her route around obstacles. Soon she saw where the path ended, bounded by a bright orange ribbon. Past the ribbon, the ground sloped sharply, seeming to fall away into darkness. That must be the way to the walking tunnel, she thought, the footpath to the City that would lead their class home, although why it was fenced off she couldn't be sure. Perhaps so small children wouldn't go inside unattended? She shivered as she took one last look at the Thames. All that heavy gray water would be weighing on whatever flimsy construction people had built to support a passageway, guaranteed to spring a leak sooner or later. Later, she hoped, her hands beginning to sweat.

Kate took a deep breath and stepped off the boardwalk,

climbed over the orange ribbon, and headed dubiously downhill along the dirt trail. She thought Fenwick had said there was an elevator—a "lift"—descending to the tunnel's entrance; perhaps, though, as with almost everything in London, the elevator shaft was under construction and this was an alternative access route. She glanced around, unsettled, as the returning drizzle pushed the trees around her out of focus.

It had been a dismal day from the very start. She'd woken early to discover the milk was sour, the bread was moldy, and the only thing for breakfast was prune yogurt. Since Willow had begun her health kick, Kate had been forced to eat things she'd never imagined people could eat. "Slugs in a blender"—that's what she called prune yogurt. In New York, her father had created amazing brunches for their bed and breakfast guests—mushroom and cheese omelets, chocolate hazelnut crepes, berry salads, and his specialty coffee.

In comparison, what Kate was eating in London was a disgrace. Willow should be hauled to prison for punishing her with this disgusting stuff. Or to the Tower. The Tower of London. Kate had gone by there on a sightseeing trip, but figured it wasn't worth the twenty pounds to go inside. The old royal prison didn't interest her at all, in spite of the sinister ravens flapping about. She sighed, her stomach growling, and wished that she'd just skipped school today, something she'd been doing with increasing regularity, unbeknownst to Willow, whose name she forged on the notes explaining various illnesses. Strep throat, bronchitis, pink eye. Kate had used stomach flu twice. She'd soon have to consult a medical dictionary, just to get some new ideas.

Her father would have noticed her skipping school and wouldn't have liked it. He had been the kind of person who paid attention. Busy with guests at the house, he'd always had time for Kate, and when she talked to him about anything, he listened. It was this, perhaps, that she missed most of all—just being listened to. Of course, you had to talk in order for someone to listen, but she didn't want to think about that now.

A sudden wind made the branches above her shake collected raindrops from their leaves, and then the sky disappeared in a hard rain that brought dirt splashing up onto Kate's ankles. She rubbed her sleeve across her eyes, her sweater—jumper, as they called it here—already soaking, and then spotted the tunnel. In spite of her unease about small spaces, Kate ran toward it, grateful for shelter. Once inside, she stood looking at the storm, conscious of the need to block out the tunnel walls that seemed to press closer the longer she lingered here. An odd smell hung about, a warm animal scent that Kate couldn't identify. She dizzily took another deep breath and then turned to face her fear as the wind pushed her deeper into the tunnel.

Kate blinked at the greenish glow that seemed to emanate

from the ground, and then stared ahead at the deep path into darkness. Her impulse was to run back into the rain, but conquering the underground path now would ensure she didn't disgrace herself later in front of anyone. She could just hear the snide remarks from Tiffany Fielding, and that rat-faced Cynthia Abbott, if they discovered her terror, the reaction to small enclosed spaces that had been with her for as long as she could remember. She blinked again, glanced at her palm, and then concentrated on taking slow, careful breaths. That was how to avert a full-blown panic attack—just keep breathing.

Kate wasn't sure when she'd developed the claustrophobia that rose at the most awkward times. Her mother's disappearance, when Kate was five, seemed to be the beginning of conscious memory, and this strange terror had been with her then. That was almost ten years ago. Could her mother have locked her up, kept her in a closet or some other small space, as punishment? Kate shivered. The idea was awful, but possible. Everything about her mother was such a mystery. Her father hadn't liked speaking of Isobel Allen, and so Kate hadn't asked the questions that plagued her. And now she couldn't ask her father about anything.

On the day her mother left, Kate had dropped a pitcher of juice on the kitchen floor. It slipped through her hands and smashed, the orange liquid streaming everywhere. Trying to sop it up with a towel, a shard of glass had pierced her palm, leaving a white scar that resembled the letter K. "K for Katherine," she'd say to herself when she could feel an anxiety attack coming on. "K for Kate." Somehow the reassurance of herself, her name, gave her strength.

I hate the way I am, she thought, spiraling into panic as she stood alone in the confines of the tunnel. *I hate myself!* She stared at her palm, the familiar breathlessness making her ears ring. She tried not to remember the way a woman with red-blonde curls and a soft voice had told her to sit on the sofa until Dad came home, said that he'd bring some Band-Aids, that everything would be all right. The woman smelled like lemons and Kate thought about the jar of lemon drops that had always been on the coffee table. She'd sucked one after another as she sat there by herself, waiting for her father, her hand wrapped up in wet paper towel, and as she remembered this, her heart gave a warning squeeze. This was her first and last memory of her mother, and she'd traced it so often over the years, she'd worn it smooth and flat as a skipping stone. Her one memory of Isobel. And after that—nothing. Isobel had simply vanished.

Kate took a hesitant step deeper into the tunnel, her eyes slowly adjusting to the absence of light. She felt misery squeeze from every pore. Was she heading toward the elevator or was this actually the path that would take her under the Thames? She had reluctantly studied both the elevator and the tunnel in Fenwick's history class, and fuzzily remembered something about two Edwardian lift shafts housed at ground level in brick rotundas with glass domes ... but maybe that was something else, something to do with the museum? The route under the Thames was all muddled up with the history of Greenwich and the items in the museum that they were supposed to be viewing. What she needed was the footpath that connected Greenwich Park to the City of London, and it didn't really matter whether or not she took an elevator to get to the footpath. She took another step forward into the dim passageway. This seemed like the right direction.

Suddenly she felt the world revolving as though she were on a ride at the fair. She dropped to her knees and then fell forward, her body flattening as if gravity were a rolling pin. Hysteria beat against her temples. She tried to move her arms and legs, and could not. She tried to catch her breath, and could not. Terror poured its black ink into her body, filling her from feet to head, and then she was conscious, for a few heady moments, of being zero, of being subtracted from herself until nothing was left. Then, jarringly, she sensed herself back inside a body with shape and form, a body that needed to breathe. She choked, her throat straining for air, and lifted her head from the dirt floor of the tunnel. There was a pinpoint of daylight in the distance. She stumbled to her feet and ran crazily, her arms and legs numb, toward the widening entrance of the tunnel.

Dazed, she emerged into daylight, expecting to see and

hear the City of London. That's where she'd be if this were the other end of the footpath under the Thames. Instead of the anticipated cityscape, she found herself in the middle of a pastoral forest, a boggy area nearby exuding a pungent smell. *Mint*, she thought, bewildered. She took a tentative step forward, then stopped when she heard the long, echoing notes of a horn. The clearing up ahead was suddenly filled with activity as horses and dogs came plunging through the undergrowth.

Her eyes feeling stretched and sore, Kate tried to take in the action before her as about a dozen men and women rode into view. It looked like a hunting party of some kind. They wore odd clothes, the men sporting long, colorful coats, puffy around the hips, overtop green or brown leggings, while the women had on long dresses. Most of the men carried bows and arrows, but there were a few spears, and the horses bore extravagantly embroidered saddle cloths, their manes and tails done up with festive ribbons. The scene looked like something from a movie.

"I've gone off my nut!" Kate breathed, borrowing a phrase from Gran. She held onto the slender trunk of a nearby tree and stared at the impossible images before her. The women's gowns were tight-waisted and of rich material, with elaborate hoods. They sat sidesaddle on their horses, their bodies twisted in what Kate thought was an awkward position, yet they managed to ride gracefully, nevertheless. On the edge of the clearing, Kate saw another girl carefully maneuvering her way among the trees. She was riding a gray pony that she quickly drew to a walk, sidestepping behind thick bushes which masked her from the hunting party. It looked as if she had just ridden quite a distance, and in her hurry was now breathless and disheveled. She seemed to be trying to avoid the hunters. She was wearing a blue-gray gown; her hood was down and she was working her waist-length auburn hair back into place while staying atop her mount. Something about her was very familiar, and Kate stared hard, trying to get a better look.

Suddenly, Kate glimpsed what the hunters were after. A muscular buck with huge antlers bounded from the trees, branches snapping with its passage. A young man a bit taller than Kate stood up in his stirrups and shot an arrow. The arrow caught the deer full in the chest and it fell to its knees, struggled to rise, and then went down in the grass, thrashing in panic. An echoing panic ran through Kate's chest. This picture no longer pleased her; unlike a movie, she couldn't pass it off as make-believe. This hunt was real! An animal was being killed, right in front of her eyes!

She tore her gaze away from the deer as the fellow's red hair, caught in the sunlight, looked as though it were on fire, a mesmerizing effect. He turned and Kate had a glimpse of his face. She'd never before seen such a look of triumph or, a moment later, such grace of motion as he slid from his horse and ran toward the deer. Something about him both interested and frightened her, and the drama of the moment made her heart beat faster. The deer tried to heave itself forward and Kate saw the bright gleam of blood. She felt sick to her stomach. This was definitely no movie.

The knife flashed in the young man's hand and he gave an excited cry, his eyes glittering as the buck shuddered and then was still. Not just still, thought Kate: dead. Had she called out, made some kind of noise, could she have saved it? Shaking, she backed further into the shadows. The hunting party yelled jubilantly and horns heralded their success. Harm and harmony, Kate thought, her legs trembling, her hands cold as ice. She saw the girl on the gray pony edge further into the concealment of the forest, trying, as Kate was trying, not to be seen. Kate retreated a little deeper into the tunnel, tripped over her own feet, and fell into a side passage that opened into an alcove. She found herself facing wide blue eyes set in a small, furry gray face. A dog! A puppy of some kind. It stumbled to its feet and tried to run, but one of its front legs buckled and it crumpled back onto the ground. As if it knew it had no chance, it sank back in the dust, eyes gleaming piteously within a band of white fur that ran across its brow and down its muzzle.

"We're both afraid," Kate said softly, "but neither of us is going to get hurt. You'll be okay. Your mama will be back soon."

She remembered with bitterness that someone had told her that once, too, a long time ago. And she was still waiting. Then she heard a low growl coming from the tunnel's opening and turned quickly, catching a glimpse of stone gray eyes and a fanged snarl. These were no dogs! She threw herself headlong into the shaft of the tunnel, desperate to get away.

The floor moved under her feet and she was once again moving out of control, a scream locked in her throat. As the force once again flattened her like dough, she heard a bone-chilling howl and her last thought before oblivion was: Wolves!

Later—and she didn't know if what had passed were minutes, hours, or some other quantity of time she couldn't measure—she found herself stumbling shakily toward the light. She made it to the original entrance of the tunnel and tumbled out into the sunshine, chest burning, hands and feet numb with dust particles pebbling her ankles like magnetic filings. The world around her seemed to be moving and she couldn't keep her balance. Falling to the grass, she lay there disoriented and sick to her stomach. Above the tree line, she could see the top of the Royal Observatory, signaling that she was once again in Greenwich Park, and the purring of nearby pigeons was oddly comforting, but her mind brimmed with a confusing mix of questions and images that had nothing to do with the sights and sounds nearby.

Finally she got her thoughts in order. Where had she been?

What exactly had she seen there? Images flashed disjointedly through her head and she rubbed at her icy hands. The wolves sorted themselves from the other already fading memories, eerily tangible. She was lucky to be alive! She got dizzily to her feet and began to make her way back along the footpath, stumbling as the ground sloped upwards toward the museum. She saw her tracks on the grass, and, on the side of the hill, her navy jacket. She headed over and snatched it up. Damp from the rain, it was still a welcome weight upon her shoulders.

"Katherine Allen," a voice growled, "where have you been!" Up ahead stood Fenwick and the class. Fenwick's dark eyes gleamed from beneath the thatch of light hair, making her look more like a greyhound than ever. Kate stared at the teacher and took a big gulp of air.

"I ... um ... I had to go to the bathroom," she stuttered, brushing her hands against her wool skirt just as she remembered she hadn't used the proper British term. "I mean, *lavatory*," she amended. Laughter rippled from her classmates, but she steadfastly went on. "And then I thought I'd just ... um ... run around for a bit until you all came out."

Fenwick's gaze never wavered from Kate's face although the teacher moved her narrow head from side to side, as if searching a scent on the breeze.

"We scoured the museum, worried that we'd left you behind," Fenwick snapped, her nostrils flaring. "Have some consideration for others the next time you decide to go for a jog. Now fall into place."

Fenwick skillfully herded the students into threes, and as they took the path again, Kate drew herself away from Tiffany and ratty Cynthia, who still had a smirk on her face as if contemplating some smart remark. For a moment, Kate thought she saw a dark shape slinking among the bushes on the other side of the path, but she blinked and the illusion—for it must have been just her imagination—was replaced by the mottled blend of autumn colors.

"Where were you?" asked Tiffany in a voice that Kate thought was intended to sound pleasant but under which she could hear the scratch of sharply manicured nails.

"Nowhere," said Kate, and looked stonily ahead, again imagining herself as Humpty Dumpty. But she wouldn't be scrambled. Boiled, that's how she wanted to act among these kids. Hard-boiled. Tiffany rolled her eyes at Cynthia, who tossed her blonde pony tail in disgust.

"*Foreigners*," she mouthed, and Kate turned away.

"Note the geodesic domes on the rotundas housing the elevator," Fenwick was directing. Kate looked with surprise at the brick building ahead. So this was the elevator. She'd apparently gone in the wrong direction and headed down toward the Thames when she should have remained on higher ground. Perhaps what she'd discovered was an old entranceway to the footpath where she'd taken a wrong turn and stumbled onto a movie set. It had to have been a movie. In her panic, she must have imagined the blood.

Kate thought again of the wolves. They had not been imagined, nor were they part of any film. She wondered, with a sharp sense of duty, if the elevator ahead accessed the same footpath where she'd encountered the wolf and her cub. Should she tell the teacher about the possible danger? She couldn't let anyone go underground if there was a mother wolf, waiting to attack. Even if its prey was Cynthia, whom she truly despised. The teacher herded them onto the large elevator and Kate caught her breath. She hated elevators. The descent, however, was mercifully swift, and, just as spots of panic began floating behind her eyes, the elevator opened onto an expanse of white tile. This, obviously, was the footpath under the Thames, although perhaps the dirt tunnel she'd been in earlier was somehow adjoining. Kate knew she had to speak up.

"The ... uh ... the tunnel might not be safe at the moment," she began, weakly.

"What do you mean?" said Fenwick, her liquid eyes fixed on Kate.

"When ... when I was down here before, I heard something. You know, there ... there might be a wolf den in here or something."

"When were you down here? You mean, just now?" Fenwick bristled, as if the idea of a student alone in the tunnel was alarming.

"Oh, no," Kate said, hurriedly. "One other time, with ... with my sister. We thought we heard wolves in the tunnel, and so I'm wondering if it's safe ..."

"Nonsense," said Fenwick. "Likely some kids having you on. You Americans certainly like to sensationalize things. There haven't been wolves in London for ages."

"But—" started Kate, and then the teacher cut her off.

"Hurry, now, let's move along," Fenwick commanded.

Well, she can go first, thought Kate. If she becomes pâté for some wild animal, it serves her right. Then we'd have to have a sub. *Supply teacher,* she mused, absently, and then, more ominously, with a rising sense of hysteria: *Don't say I didn't warn you.*

"Forward," said Fenwick, her narrow head turning one way, then the other. "Towards the City!"

"Please, Miss Fenwick, I have to use the lavatory," Amandella called out, her nasal voice echoing against the tile walls of the footpath.

"Not now, Miss Hingenbottom," answered the teacher. "You must wait until we reach the tube stop at the other side of the Thames."

Kate moved unsteadily along the flagstones of the immense walkway that was to take them back to the City of London. She knew the sounds she'd heard were not the result of kids playing tricks. She had seen and heard real wolves, although this part of the tunnel certainly seemed safe enough.

"Only in England," she mused, staring at the glazed white tile surrounding them. Clearly it was lavatory material, and she could see it stretching ahead for what looked like miles and miles. Rather than a transit tunnel, it looked like a gargantuan bathroom. Or some kind of morgue. Kate took a long, shaky breath. A strong scent of disinfectant completed the impression and she wrinkled her nostrils, stealing glances at the other girls, none of whom seemed the slightest bit uncomfortable about the possibility of being pickled alive.

Cynthia and Tiffany whispered to each other and stole glances at Kate, while Tiffany at the same time applied tulip-red lipstick to her own puckered lips. Amandella blew her nose on a long string of toilet paper she'd obviously had balled up in her pocket for quite some time. Parvana and Navjiit giggled about something. One of the quieter students—a pretty girl named Hannah—furiously scribbled in a notebook as she walked along, halting every now and then to complete a sentence.

But as Kate moved further into the walkway, she wasn't thinking of the other girls. Instead, the children's rhyme beat a steady staccato against her temples: *All the king's horses, and all the king's men, couldn't put Humpty together again.*

3
William

Young William Fitzroy stopped and leaned his lanky frame against the cool stones for a moment before opening the gate in the wall. Although the morning was cool, the burden he carried in his cloak was making him sweat just a little. He entered the garden and then used his hip to push the gate shut. There. He had done it. So far his little bundle was safe and sound. If he could just get it into the shed at the far end of the garden, things might be all right.

William was tired, a thick, aching exhaustion that filled the very marrow of his bones. He had not been resting well, worries thrumming in his brain until the darkness was all but consumed by dawn, before sleep came to the rescue. Yawning, he headed past old raspberry canes and rhubarb stalks, wondering at his own courage in defying the Crown. Wolves had been outlawed long ago. Was he really going to disobey his King and try to save this small creature? Warmth from the cub seeped through the cloth into his arms. Perhaps it was the last of its kind in England. He strengthened his resolve. I am obliged to do what is right, he told himself. In spite of the consequences.

William knew no one entered this little garden, abandoned for so long. Across the road from the Friars' Church, it was a solitary spot surrounded by the low stone wall half hidden by thick, gleaming holly and tendrils of climbing ivy. It had rained earlier that day and the pale green ivy leaves gave off such a scent that he stopped for a minute just to breathe the heavenly sweetness. The garden had once been tended by Princess Margaret, but four years ago she had married King James and gone to Scotland. He supposed that since then the place had become overgrown and forgotten, the tools in the shed untouched, judging by the brambles that stretched over the doorstep of the shed and the cobwebs strung across the frame.

He'd come across the garden in one of the fitful, wandering moods that overcame him now and then as he pondered his state here in the royal court, haunted by his responsibilities to young Prince Henry, the Duke of York, as well as his dual allegiance to Father, locked up in the Tower by King Henry VII on suspicion of treason. Not that Father had done anything wrong. Somehow, if it took forever, William was determined to find a way to prove his father's innocence and set him free.

Quickly, in case someone discovered him and confiscated the little animal, he kicked away the weeds and thrust open the door of the shed, depositing the cub on an empty sack in a corner where it quickly stirred and came gingerly awake. The interior of the shed smelled musty, but at least it was dry. As William went about finding a bowl, he muttered comfort to the creature and, when he brought back fresh water from the stream that ran alongside the garden, the poor thing lifted its head and managed a brief drink. Without the strength to stand, it soon fell back onto the straw and sank into a restless sleep.

It reminded him of the orphan lambs he'd tended by the dozen every spring. Mothers dead or reluctant to care for their babies, and the young ones weak, yet so desperate for nourishment, they'd push themselves to stay alert for the goat's milk he'd squeeze into their mouths. You could usually tell from the eyes whether they had the spark to hang onto life, and that made you work harder to save them. Once they'd learned to take the milk from a pail, things got much easier. He wondered who would be caring for them next spring. Maybe Charlotte? He hoped his little sister wasn't worked too much in his absence. He also hoped his mother had time to encourage Charlotte's reading. Charlotte was quick, even quicker than he had been at that age. Before he'd left home, she'd already learned all the psalms in Latin.

William sat beside the cub in deep contemplation, feeling his own courage slipping away. What good was he in court? A palace was no setting for a farmer, which was his calling just as it was the calling of his father and brothers. "Farm Boy," Prince Henry called him in jest. He missed the plain meals, the fresh air, and, most of all, he missed his family. Yet his duty, he knew, was here at Placentia. At least in this location he was close to his father. When the royal household moved on from Greenwich to a new residence, opening the Palace of Placentia for cleaning, he wasn't sure what he'd do. At any rate, it was useless sitting here worrying, when he should be studying Latin. He got to his feet. Time waited for no man.

"Get some rest, laddie," William whispered to the cub. "It'll do you a great bit of good. I'll be back at dusk with bread and milk for your supper." He shivered in the cool damp air as he left the hut, crossed the garden, and opened the wooden gate. Then, as an afterthought, he ducked back into the garden, quickly returning to the hut and arranging his cloak over the sleeping form. It was the best he could do. The rest of the day would be taken up with lessons, beginning with Latin, a subject he detested. But soon he would return.

"Amo, amas, amat, amamus, amatis, amunt," William muttered, fastening the door behind him. Or was the correct plural form *amant*? Perhaps the prince would assist him. Prince Henry excelled at Latin, and, more often than not, deftly corrected William's conjugations before their tutor detected the errors. God bless the Prince, for there was nothing their tutor despised more than vocabulary mistakes. *Charlotte would do better,* William thought, wondering, as he had often wondered, why girls weren't given the formal education that boys were.

Three notes of a dove rang mournfully in the garden. William stopped to listen for any sound from the shed, but all was silent. The cub would sleep and then perhaps later it could be persuaded to eat and drink more substantially. The front leg was the problem; perhaps William could borrow some of the salve they used on the horses to see if it would help. The dove called again and sadness welled up in William's throat. He swallowed hard and headed through the gate and down the lane. Life wasn't fair, but you had to do what you could. *The Lord ruleth me,* he thought, the words of the psalm rising in a distant memory of Charlotte's clear voice. *The Lord ruleth me: and I shall want nothing. He hath set me in a place of pasture. He hath brought me up, on the water of refreshment. He hath converted my soul.*

As William went through the guard room and into the palace proper, a warm feeling crept over him. Even if he couldn't help Father just now, at least he could care for this animal, and, God willing, return it to health. It was too young to be alone in the forest. He wondered what had happened to its mother. Likely hunted down with all the other wolves in England. William shuddered. He hated the thought of any living thing suffering. But had he done the right thing? It could mean disaster if he were caught.

William scratched at a spot on his neck. Blasted fleas, eating him alive in the few hours he managed to sleep. When God created fleas, it must have been an accident. Wolves, now, they were part of the chain of everything. Without natural predators, other species would swell their ranks. Rabbits, even deer, would overrun things. As far as the wolves went, William thought superstition was to blame for their bad reputation. He'd heard stories about wolves, of course—what farmer hadn't? He also knew that his father had never actually lost a sheep to a wolf. Stories and fear could make people do terrible deeds.

There had been a cunning woman consulted in the village about the missing royal communion cloth. He'd heard the servants talking about it, gossiping about how this woman was a known sorcerer, and surely she could say who stole it. She was the same cunning woman the palace had consulted about the sweating sickness, when it seemed a few courtiers were getting sick a fortnight ago. William shivered. He loathed illness as much as Prince Henry did, and hoped he himself would never be affected, but, unlike the Prince, William never shunned those who needed a strong shoulder or a cup of ale. Jesus himself had never turned his back, and so nor would he—a lowly follower. Of course, the Prince had to take care because his was an important life, and someday many people would depend on his rule. William's life was less significant, he knew. Still ... it was significant to him.

"Farm Boy!" said Prince Henry, grinning broadly when William entered the study. "You're late. I thought we might have to send the hounds out for you!"

"Sorry," William responded, grateful for the Prince's goodwill. He scratched the spot on his neck, now bloody, and then brushed the hair out of his eyes. "Good hunting this morning?"

"Yes, very excellent hunting, my friend. We hung one big buck and spied two others." William felt a quick rush of envy at the Prince's prowess, although he himself didn't care much for hunting. Somehow, in his company, the Prince made everyone feel this way—lucky to be looked upon kindly, and in awe of his presence. William wasn't sure how he did it.

"I'll be out again tomorrow—hope we do as well," Henry continued. "Saw a wolf, too, horrible mangy creature. Took a shot, but somehow its carcass eluded us. I'll have to pay a visit to MacQueen on Saturday and see what he has to say for himself."

William sat down and didn't reply. The Prince's loathing of wolves was based on superstition and not on any real evidence, quite unlike the way Henry usually formed his opinions. Best not to talk about it, for one couldn't contradict the heir to the throne. All of God's creatures had a right to dignity, and wolves were no different, in spite of their perceived threat to the King's lands. William considered the cub, concealed in the shed, and tightened his mouth in a firm line. It might be one of the last wolves in England for all he knew. Alone and separated from its family. For a moment, William thought of his own family and how, just as the wolf was alone, he himself was alone, here at court—small and powerless. Just then the door opened and three other boys stormed in, followed hot on their heels by the tutor.

"All right, young masters, take a seat, take a seat," said the elderly teacher, rubbing his hands together, the white hairs on his thumbs bobbing up and down. William wondered joylessly if perhaps this old scholar wasn't descended from a troll, or worse.

"Before the conjugations we'll have the definitions," continued the tutor enthusiastically, white froth already appearing in the corners of his mouth. "And anyone not responding will write out lines."

"I'd rather lie in a ditch and be bowled with turnips," muttered William. Henry shot him a wink and the other boys sent each other agonized glances.

"Vocare!" the tutor crowed, pronouncing the "v" as a "w" as with all Latin words.

"To call!" the boys said in unison.

"Pugnare!"

"To fight."

"Videre?"

"To conquer," said two of the boys, faintly, while the others remained silent.

"Wrong!" sang the tutor. "Videre, vides, vedet, vedemus ... to see! You see?" he grinned at his own lofty pun, displaying blueish gums with uneven yellow teeth.

"We'll start with that conjugation," he said firmly. "On paper, twenty times over, begin!"

William groaned inwardly. The definitions were tedious, but having to write out conjugations was even worse. He knew better than to show his discomfort, as he had often experienced the tutor's quick temper. William often got a beating on account of the Duke, for if Prince Henry was caught in error, the other boys—and William in particular—were required to take, on Prince Henry's behalf, the blows of a stout stick. No one, as far as he knew, disciplined the Duke of York. Being a prince had some advantages, although William himself would not have appreciated the fussing Prince Henry bore over his person.

William's mind darted back to the old woman and the servants' tales. They'd said she was a cunning woman for sure, and could prevent cows from giving milk, and cause ewes to die in labor. William was suspicious of these accusations. His farm background told him that animals often strayed from human requirements—nature's way of extracting power from humans, or so his father said. Still, if she could bring back the Church's communion cloth, that would be a blessing.

Now he picked up his pen and dipped the nib into the ink, tapping it gently so it wouldn't blot. As he started with the conjugation, he thought of the wolf cub and nodded to himself. First, he'd better get through Latin and French, tedious as they were. And hunting practice, where he would have to struggle with the bow and arrow. Prince Henry was the best hunter and thus the bar was high for the rest of them. But after the evening meal, William would go back and see what he could do to help the cub. Possibly the wound had poisoned the whole of the creature, and it would already be dead. But possibly it could be mended. Under every ill, there was something—a wound, or a festering sore—feeding the trouble. He knew you had to cure the underlying cause before you could make things right. *Might as well be hung for a sheep as a lamb,* he thought wryly, steeling himself for the task that lay ahead.

4
The invitation

As Kate got off the bus at King's Cross, she kept thinking about the incredible experience she'd had. As with a complicated math problem, she turned the details over and over in her mind, hoping things would balance. The explanation—that she'd come across a movie set—went quickly out of favor. Things did not die on movie sets, and that deer was definitely dead. Dead as a doornail, Gran would say. She shuddered at the memory of its fallen form, its final attempt to rise, and then the sense of life extinguished. And the young man's glittering eyes at his triumph over the poor creature. Could she have stumbled on a traditional hunt of some kind? In a part of London she'd not seen before? These ideas did not seem plausible, but there had to be a good explanation. Suddenly, she heard a low voice behind her.

"You're home early, aren't you, luv?"

It was Hal, a boy from the sixth form, striding up beside her. He was a few years older than she was and totally cute. She'd seen him around the school and she knew all the girls admired him. Once, at the school's tube stop, he'd teased her about being too fond of a library book. She remembered the incident clearly because of the way the other girls responded.

"Look at Big Apple," Cynthia had whispered, her mean little eyes dancing. "Has she always been that red?"

"Ever since she fell off the tree," Tiffany responded.

If they were jealous then, they'd be really jealous now, thought Kate. What could she say to this guy? She wished she could think of something smart. He seemed to be coming from the King's Cross tube station and she wondered what he was doing. She'd never seen him in this neighborhood.

"Do you live around here?" she blurted.

"No, but I'll walk you home." He seemed to be assessing her, his eyes roving from her feet to her head.

She started walking and he kept step beside her, putting a hand on the small of her back.

"A nice afternoon if it doesn't rain," he said. As if in answer, a few drops fell, and then a few more, until it was drizzling steadily and Kate picked up her pace. What could she say to this guy? And why was he walking with her?

"See you," she said, finally, stopping in front of her building. She agonized at her awkwardness, but Hal was looking up at the etched stonework, the carved words *London House for Overseas Graduates* standing out clearly in the dusky afternoon light.

"Funny name for flats," he said.

"It's university apartments," she said, and then, using the British term, "Flats. It's a residence for people who already have a university degree from somewhere else."

"You don't say," he said. "So what degree do you have?"

"Oh! It's not me," she said. "It's my sister. Willow. She finished her B.A. from New York State, and then she worked as an understudy in the Blue Man Theater Company, and now she's studying here at RADA."

"The Royal Academy of Dramatic Arts," said Hal. "Blimey. And the Blue Man troop? They're famous world over! Did she shave her head and paint it blue and everything?"

"Yes," said Kate, trying to relax. "It looked really funny, all bumpy where her hair used to be, and the blue paint was pretty radical. She's still got short hair, but nothing like it used to be."

"Must have been quite a sight," he said. "Like a blue Sno Cone."

"Well, not exactly," said Kate, her awkwardness returning. Whatever Willow did to her looks, she always managed to be chic and artsy. Kate took a furtive glance at herself, at the way her coat puffed out over her wool skirt making her look about two hundred pounds.

"She's doing *Henry VIII*," she blurted, grabbing for a thread of conversation.

"She's playing Henry?" asked Hal.

"No, of course not!" said Kate before she realized that Hal was teasing, and then she felt silly for missing the joke.

"I've often thought of trying my hand at acting," he continued.

Kate stared at him, unable to think of what to say next.

"All the men in my family have been good-lookers," he said, winking at her. "I suppose I'd be a natural talent."

"Oh, it takes—" Kate started and stopped. She was going to say it takes more than looks, but that wouldn't sound very polite. "Willow likes acting," she amended, feebly. "A lot."

There was an uncomfortable silence. "In fact," Kate went on, desperately, "she ... she really loves acting." Why couldn't she think of something amazing to say, something that would make him fall madly and hopelessly in love with her forever? Instead, her mind was as soggy as the gray sky overhead.

"Today's Friday, isn't it?" he said. "I'll pick you up at seven if you can be ready on the dot," he continued, his grin carving a charming dimple into one cheek.

It wasn't a question, but Kate, blushing wildly, started to answer.

"Well, I can't tonight—"

"Of course you *can*," said Hal, and looked at her with his twinkling blue eyes. "The question is whether you *will*. I think you should—unless you have something better to do?" His gaze seemed to see right into her brain, and the dull evening that stretched before her. "But maybe you're busy with one of your stuffy books. *The Properties of Physics*, maybe?"

Kate opened her mouth but no words came out. How had Hal remembered her library book? It must have made quite an impression.

"Do you ... I mean, have you read ..." Kate began.

"I have a good memory for things I like," Hal interrupted, as if reading her mind.

"Do you like physics?" she asked, stupidly, hearing him snort with laughter.

"Only in principle," he responded. "I don't like books as much as the people who carry them about. Come on, then, it's Friday night. You know you've got nothing better to do. I'll meet you at the corner at seven." And that settled it. They had a date. A date! Kate wished she could think of something interesting to say.

"Don't be late, now. Seven sharp," Hal told her. He stepped forward—was he going to kiss her? Then Kate somehow lost her balance and toppled against the black iron fence that surrounded the front garden. She righted herself just in time to catch another wink and a grin before Hal turned and sauntered back the way they had come, eventually disappearing around the corner.

Her legs felt like limp spaghetti. He was so good looking!

And so much older. And ... and she was so dismal. She wished she were like Willow: tall, slim, stylish. But, she sighed, she was only herself. Dumb and dumpy. *Dumpty!* she christened herself wryly.

Tonight, she resolved, brushing her wet cheek, she'd be more fun. Boys liked it if you acted cheerful. She had seen the other girls giggling at school, flirting with guys they liked. She practiced a small giggle out loud. It sounded so squeaky that she despaired of it ever impressing Hal. "Can't make a silk purse out of a sow's ear," Gran would say. Sighing, Kate opened the gate, wishing she could just jump in the shower and come out a different person.

She wondered if Hal had been waiting for her at the station. She knew he didn't live around here because he always took the tube in the other direction, so he must have been hanging around King's Cross for some purpose. The thought of him lurking in the shadows gave her an odd feeling. But how else was he to find her? They hardly ever saw each other by chance. A warm rush of pleasure filled her chest and her heart beat faster. He was at least two years older and all the girls at school were crazy about him. But why would he be interested in her? She picked the dirt out from under her thumbnail. Maybe he just had a thing for short, plump redheads. As she stood thinking about how cute he was—his red-gold hair, his broad shoulders—her eye fell on the withered roses that hung their heads against the fence.

A frost this early in October, she thought, surprised, touching the wrinkled petals. *A killing frost,* Gran would say. Gran was one of the reasons her father had let Willow come to London in the first place—because she could spend weekends with Gran in Brighton and have the influence of family, as Dad put it. Dad had been pretty protective. And then when he'd died, Gran had thought it best that Kate come to live in London, as well, and Willow had agreed. "Sisters need each other," Gran had said. "But you must stay with me in Brighton on weekends when you can."

Gran had selected the private Camden school—promised Kate that it would give her the education she required to go on in whatever field she wanted. It was expensive. Kate had seen the financial statements on Willow's desk. But that didn't make her grateful. She just didn't care about school. And as for future plans—it was hard enough taking life day by day without trying to think about the years to come. Since the car accident that killed her father, she'd felt like a piece of cotton fluff, whirled this way and that in the wind until eventually ... eventually she, too, would vanish. Just as the people she loved had vanished—first her mother and then her father.

She pushed open the heavy door to the building and stepped inside and, for the third time that day, thought about disappearing and what a relief that would be. It wasn't fair that her dad had died, and it was more than unfair to find herself stuck with life in this stupid place, going to that stupid school. And now, she had an evening ahead with this totally cute guy, and she was sure to blow it. Whatever had attracted him was sure to evaporate once he spent any time with her.

She plodded up the worn marble stairs, deciding that the exercise couldn't hurt. Her thoughts returned to the cost of the school. A check arrived from Gran every few weeks that would certainly be helping fund her education. Kate had seen Willow open the envelopes, purse her lips, and tuck the slips of paper into her wallet. Sometimes when the bank statements arrived, Kate could tell her sister was worried. But Willow was twenty-three, old enough to take care of things.

Did Fenwick actually get paid more for working there because it was a private school? Kate bit her lip in disgust, stopping for a moment on the landing to catch her breath. That greyhound of a woman had senses unknown to humankind, and wherever her salary went, it wasn't going toward personal hygiene. Fenwick often smelled of B.O. and everyone knew the teacher passed gas in class.

As she navigated the last flight, Kate wondered whether she'd be as slim as Willow if she always took the stairs. It was more than exercise that did it for Willow, she guessed. Stress used up a lot of calories, and Willow fretted about a lot of things. At first, Kate thought it was going to be easy living with Willow. But Willow quickly proved to be more protective even than Dad. You had to tell her where you were going. You had to tell her when you'd be back. And you had to get all your homework done, every detail, well ahead of deadlines. For a while, Willow had tried to make Kate run, as she had in New York. Training had been part of her lifestyle then but, with her short legs, Kate knew she'd never be a track star. Why bother?

As Kate opened the doorway to the second floor, she pulled off the navy jacket, damp from the rain, and wondered what Willow would say about her date with Hal. With some misgivings, she realized she didn't even know Hal's last name. But Willow would be at the theater. If Kate was back home early enough, the date would be her secret. Nobody would have to know—not Willow, not Gran, not anyone.

5
The memories

Kate pushed the large gold key into the lock but it stuck, as usual, when she tried to turn it. She grabbed the door handle and rattled it as hard as she could. Stupid door—why was it always such a pain? In New York, her dad could have fixed this easily, but here, you had to apply for a repairman from Reception and then wait about fifteen years.

"Here, let me help with that." Kate jerked around. It was their tall, angular neighbor, Martin Brown. He'd come so quietly down the hallway that Kate hadn't heard him approach. "It's simpler if you turn the key instead of the door." Martin Brown smiled. Then they both laughed when, with a flick of his wrist, he turned the key and opened the door as easily as if it had been unlocked to start with.

"Well," he said, stepping back toward his own flat. "Be seeing you."

"Yeah," said Kate, looking at his jet black hair with admiration. It was sleek and shiny, like a raven's wing. Then she suddenly remembered his line of work. "You study history, right?" she asked.

"That's my field, yes," he said. "Although I'm not exactly an expert on general knowledge, you know, just things specific to my subject area ..."

"I'm ... I'm interested in wolves," she blurted. "Like, why everyone says there aren't any in England."

"Wolves," said Martin Brown slowly. He gave her a quizzical glance. "The English people exterminated the wolves a very long time ago, likely before the 1500s. Why do you ask?"

Kate could feel herself flushing. "I'm ... uh ... writing something for our school newspaper. I'm supposed to find out some interesting facts."

Martin Brown turned his own key in its lock and stood for a moment, muttering to himself. Kate noticed how his sleeves were too long, his wrinkled coat hanging on him like ruffled feathers. "Wolves ... an interesting subject ..."

"Well ..." said Kate, when it didn't seem as if he was going to offer any new information, "I'll be seeing you." She looked at his door to see if the other name was still on it, and it was. Martin and Ellen Brown. Too bad, she thought. Martin Brown was just the right height for Willow. And his bright black hair would be such an interesting contrast to Willow's blondness.

“One can’t be a hundred percent certain ...” Martin Brown said, surprisingly. “Not a hundred percent certain. About anything, really. I have an interesting book on the Renaissance if you ever—”

“I ... um ... I have to go in, now, because I probably have to do the dishes,” Kate interrupted. The last thing she wanted to do was read any history books. She stepped inside and quickly shut the door behind her, leaving Martin Brown in the hallway. She wondered if she’d been too abrupt, but it was a little late now to worry about it.

Once inside, Kate hung up her wet jacket. Out of habit, she sniffed the air in the flat, although, as usual, there were no comforting smells of cooking to welcome her. Willow, of course, had already gone to the theater. Back home in New York in the other life she’d had, their father liked to make rich pasta suppers that included lots of herbs and mushrooms, savory sauces that scented the whole house with mouthwatering goodness. Although it was billed as a bed and breakfast, there were meals offered almost any time of day. Now Kate wandered into their tiny, airless kitchen and looked around. Her father would have hated it here. For one thing, when he cooked, he used a lot of shelf space. In contrast, she and Willow barely had room to set down their cereal bowls, and then there was no space to sit and eat, just room to stand at the counter. There was a little table in the living room but they hardly ever used it.

It was her father's deluxe fare that won over even the most reluctant of paying guests: afternoon snacks composed of hot scones, cream, and raspberry jam, cold chocolate coffee of his own invention, and preserved oranges. Their house, close to Broadway and all the shows, had been ideal for sight-seers. And her father had been the perfect tour guide, always willing to give advice, with stories to tell about various local haunts. Less than four months ago, she had been in that life, unaware of how lucky she was. And unaware, too, of how quickly things could change. She thought with a sudden flood of emotion of the rough feel of her father's cheek when she bent down to hug him after a hard day. He always smelled of aftershave, a clean, tangy odor that made her think of Christmas because of the evergreen scent. And he always had time for her.

They'd been on the expressway, driving home from the dental surgeon's where she'd had a wisdom tooth removed. Her father had fiddled with the radio and then suddenly given a strange kind of moan and veered out into the other lane. With practiced ease, Kate skipped thinking about the rest, fastening on the bit she let herself explore. A heart attack, the doctor had said. Surprising in a man so young. Possibly he could have been saved if he had been wearing his seat belt. Possibly not.

Why hadn't he been wearing his seat belt? She couldn't remember him ever not wearing it, but then she hadn't really checked. She'd been wearing hers. The perfect safety commercial, father and daughter heading home, but only the daughter makes it. The grim reality of black and white, a necessity for the image at the end of the commercial, thought Kate, torturing herself. A bride, walking alone down the aisle. Tears sprung to her eyes as she pictured herself in such a scene.

How old was he? Kate stood alone in the dark little kitchen, trying to remember. I don't even know what year he was born, she thought. I don't know anything about him at all. He had curly hair. Hazel eyes. An aquiline nose. These separate features disconnected and, for a moment, Kate couldn't even recall his face. He was my dad, the parent who raised me, and I know as little about him as I do about Isobel, she thought, desperately. She reached for a bag of cookies that was in the cupboard and opened them, chewing absently as she walked out of the kitchen. *Biscuits,* she thought, superimposing the English term on top of the American word. Funny how something could simultaneously be two different things, depending on where it was.

The flat was eerily quiet. Kate wandered through the rooms, noticing the newspapers and rubbish strewn about. What did it matter how messy their place was? What did anything matter? She went back into the kitchen. There was a pot of soup on the stove and a note taped to the cupboard that said: *eat it or else.* Nice little domestic welcome, thought

Kate. Willow's notes were as loud and demanding as if she were there in person, bellowing.

Kate sniffed at the soup and made a face. Split pea and potato, her least favorite of all. With something like chicken noodle, the ingredients were predictable and familiar. But what exactly was a split pea? Did they grow like that or did people go around factory kitchens mashing them to bits? She ate another cookie and pondered the experience of peas.

Willow had been on a soup kick for at least three weeks and kept announcing that it was the cheapest and healthiest way to get their quota of vitamins. Kate shuddered. I'd rather eat cockroaches than this slop, she thought. She'd always been suspicious of things that had vegetables in perfect tiny squares. A potato was never meant to be a regular hexahedron, she thought, drawing on geometry class. Or, in other words, a Platonic solid. She wandered into the living room, where the question mark she'd drawn on the sooty wall was still visible. Then she went into the bathroom to wash up and saw a dozen or so thin dark shapes darting for cover behind pictures and down drains. Something—their toenails, perhaps—made a hissing sound.

At least the London roaches were tidy creatures and she saw them only in the bathroom, unlike the huge cockroaches they had back in New York around the kitchen drains. Those must have evolved to survive our winters, Kate thought with a wry smile, tying her hair back with an elastic band. Her father had called them kittens so he and Kate could talk without alerting paying visitors to the pests.

"One of the kittens was under the kitchen sink this morning," he'd say, warm eyes laughing, or he'd wave a hand that had just been running through his tousled curls: "Katie, my darling, you won't believe how that naughty kitten got into the guest bathroom!" Kate would stealthily wait until the guests had gone out for the day, and then she'd set the roach trap. They'd worked as a team, she and her dad, and she ached in his absence. In this new life, it seemed as if everything she did was solitary. And all her memories, even the good ones, had been invaded by a kind of secret sadness that filled the cracks and crannies of her storied past with blue. How temporary things were! And then the worst thought of all, the one that had been hammering at her for what seemed like years, settled against her chest, beating its heavy wings. What good was living at all if, in the end, death swept everything away?

She thought of her mother and the old bitterness surfaced. At least her father had a reason for not being with her. But her mother ... the way Isobel had disappeared, with such finality, was unforgivable. The old thoughts—that maybe she, Kate, had made her mother want to leave them—made her swallow hard. The idea always managed to embed a lingering ache in her throat, as if she'd swallowed something hard—a pebble, or a penny. How bad had she been when she was five? Other than breaking the juice pitcher, she couldn't remember. And her fear of small spaces—was it caused by her mother?

Turning on the water, she stared at her hands, carefully turning over the left one to display the scar. *K for Kate.* "K for Kate," she repeated to herself, finally breaking the hold of the dismal thoughts. She washed her face, the cloth coming away with gray streaks from the London smog.

She went into her room and changed out of her school uniform, and then wandered back into the kitchen where she shoved the soup pot into the fridge and then deliberated. A big jar of lemon spread looked tempting, and Kate had often seen Willow smearing some on toast, but she passed it by. Lemon had a peculiar effect on her, bringing on the same panic as small spaces. She ate another cookie. The box of sweets above the stove tempted her; with sudden resolve, she rejected them. If she kept on gaining weight, she'd need all new clothes, and who was going to pay for that? Instead, she chose another container of stupid yogurt and, standing at the counter, ate it with a plastic spoon. Then she sat in the living room, staring furiously at the question mark she'd etched on the wall. What had happened in the tunnel? It had been some kind of amazing journey, and her mind felt bruised with possibilities. If only she had a simple equation that would explain everything.

She recalled what that physics book said about order:

Organizing things uses energy, which is released into the environment, causing disorder. She thought she understood. The more she tried to figure things out, the more confused and upset she would be. The theory made sense. But how could you stop putting order to things? She would have liked to look back in the physics book for answers but it wasn't on the shelf. She must have returned it to the library. She threw down the plastic spoon and chucked the empty yogurt cup into the kitchen garbage. Then she reached for the box of sweets, eating first the green ones, then the red.

Finally, disgusted with herself, she put the box away and decided to phone Gran. She needed to make an excuse for not going up to Brighton this weekend. It wasn't that she didn't like her grandmother. It was more about getting close to someone who might let her down that was the real problem. Best not to rely on anyone, so if they ... disappeared, it wouldn't really matter. Gran answered on the first ring, sounding a bit startled, as if Kate had caught her by surprise. When Kate asked if everything was all right, Gran's voice had a hollow sound, although her words were reassuring.

"How's Patch?" Kate asked. Patch was her grandmother's golden spaniel, and since Grandfather had died a few years ago, the dog was her dearest companion—"next to my girls." Often Gran would hold the phone down to dog level, something Kate thought bizarre and a bit childish. Patch, however, could usually be counted on to whimper a response.

"Sorry, luv, he's out for an evening stroll around the garden. Ta for asking. I'd best not talk long, for I've got to keep an eye."

"I'm sure he's fine just walking in the garden, isn't he?" Kate asked, replacing the immediate image of an American vegetable garden with the grass and shrubbery that defined gardens here in England. "I mean, you've got that stone wall ..."

"Oh yes, the wall's sound, my dear. No worries about that. We've just had some doings here that make it important to take care. Glad you're in London, now, where things are safe."

Safe? Kate almost dropped the phone. She couldn't believe Gran had just said that. Safe, when all Gran had ever said about London was that it was a dangerous city, especially after dark. She and Willow were always telling her to be careful, to be cautious, to be sure and lock the door at all times!

"What's the matter?" Kate blurted.

"Oh, not anything, really," Gran said, her voice a bit uncertain. After a pause, she went on: "I've just been busy, luv. Selling a bit of old furniture and other trappings I don't really need. Wore myself out just a bit, I think ..." Her voice trailed off and then she added, "And there ... well, there's been some funny goings on here at night, you know. Wild dogs, or something, running in a pack, taking people by surprise and such."

"Taking people by surprise? You mean attacking people?"

"Well, not exactly. There haven't been injuries, but we're all being a little extra wary. Not to worry, though. It'll all work out. You just have to believe and it'll all work out. But I'd best go now, dearie, so if there isn't anything else ... I'll go and put the kettle on. I'll tell Patch you said hello. Ta for calling."

"Wait," started Kate. "What year was—" but she heard the line go dead. Gran had hung up before she could ask the question about her father's birth date. It didn't matter, anyway. What use was history? It couldn't bring him back. Nothing could bring him back.

As she hung up the phone, an odd feeling of dread filled Kate's stomach. She'd never heard Gran sound so distant. It was like she wasn't really thinking about their conversation at all. And it wasn't like Gran not to try and cajole Kate and Willow into a visit. She'd been after Kate to learn bridge so they could play as partners with a couple of neighbors. Kate looked out the window into darkness and a shiver ran down her spine. Wild dogs ... or wolves? Had they been seeing wolves in Brighton? Martin Brown's words came back: "You can't be a hundred percent certain about anything."

Wolves. *Wolves.* Kate scanned her memory for what she knew about them, hoping to piece things together in a plausible way. Maybe she had stumbled into an excavation site that wolves had extended by digging. She remembered that wolves lived in dens, and possibly what she'd found was a wolf den. As soon as this idea occurred to her, she discarded it. What she'd been in was certainly not a den—it was much too large.

Wolves live and hunt in packs, led by the dominant alpha male, she recalled. Wolves are fierce and bloodthirsty. In some countries, Norway for example, people think they're a harbinger of death. Kate thought of her dad, but *harbinger* meant *predictor*, and Dad was already gone. And he wasn't, she added silently to herself, ever coming back. She thought of her mother and felt again as if a stone were lodged in her throat. Caught in a swirl of gray thoughts, Kate suddenly remembered her tracks earlier that day across the soft damp grass of Greenwich Park. They had lasted just long enough to give her a sense of direction back to the Naval College. But by now, the tracks would have vanished.

She took a deep breath and wandered in and out of her bedroom, and then into Willow's room. Willow had some freaky masks hanging on the walls and lots of bright, gaudy jewelry strewn on the bureau. Her closet was stuffed with clothes. Tall leopard skin boots poked out, along with a short purple miniskirt, a filmy white blouse, a Hawaiian shirt, a black leather jacket, and two mismatched tennis shoes.

Kate felt the blueness of another memory when she saw those shoes. She and Willow used to play lots of tennis together when they were younger. Willow had won a scholarship to a dance academy when she was thirteen, but she'd been home on weekends and for longer holidays, too, when they'd often had time for a match. Their dad had taught them the rules and it had been fun to play singles, with Dad sometimes joining in as a competitor. Tall and athletic, he had always clearly dominated, until two summers ago when Kate had finally beaten Willow, their eight year age difference suddenly irrelevant. Then it was between Kate and her dad, and she knew that if she practiced hard enough, she could beat him, too.

Kate sighed. Willow didn't have any time for tennis, now. And even if she had, her bossy attitude would wreck everything. Kate felt a little pang of guilt, remembering the recent battles she'd had with her sister, but quickly shrugged it off. The fighting was Willow's fault. Nagging and cross, her sister was such a pain. Twenty-three going on eighty-five.

A few posters were up on Willow's bedroom walls. Actors, mostly, but only a few Kate recognized. And one actress—Willow's role model—Audrey Hepburn. Kate had seen Hepburn only once, on TV in a special movie presentation of *Breakfast at Tiffany's.*

Willow looks nothing like Audrey Hepburn, Kate thought, scrutinizing the picture. Willow did have a big voice, even when she wasn't on stage. Just not big hair. She wore a wig in the production they were doing now, when she played Anne somebody-or-other to another actor's Henry VIII. Kate had listened distractedly as Willow had told her the Shakespearian version of the history lesson, but most of what Willow had said went in one ear and out the other. Kate supposed she'd have to see the play on Preview Night next week. It was going to be boring.

Lying over a chair in the closet was a long, blue gown that Kate thought looked rather familiar. When she lifted it up, the fabric clung to her, soft and inviting. It wasn't yet hemmed, but pinned at the cuffs and skirt as well as down one side. Even without it being finished, Kate could tell it wasn't meant for her tall, slim sister. This dress was of a Tudor design, similar to the dress Willow was to wear in her show, but definitely created for someone of Kate's stature.

Kate started pulling the dress over her head, just to see how it looked. If she'd been wearing this in that place at the end of the tunnel, she'd have totally blended in. As the fabric pressed tightly around her shoulders, she felt her breath catch in her throat. Quickly she squirmed out of the dress, the old feeling of claustrophobia catching her by surprise. Carefully replacing the outfit inside the closet, she wondered briefly if it might be meant for her, and then shook her head. Why would her sister give her a Tudor dress? Anyway, it was too tight.

Kate slipped out of Willow's room and closed the door. Better mind my own business, she thought, her face burning. She looked at the clock. It was almost seven! Hal would be out there waiting! She ran to the bathroom, splashed water on her face, although that just made her hot cheeks redder, and shoved the elastic from her pony tail into her jeans' pocket, letting the soft, auburn hair swirl free against her neck.

As Kate picked up the key from the table in the hall, she deliberated. Then, stuffing her underground pass and a few bills into her pocket, she decided not to take a purse. Might get stolen. Her navy jacket was still wet and, without a second thought, Kate ran into Willow's room and pulled the black leather coat from the closet. What Willow didn't know wouldn't hurt her.

Then Kate left the flat, carefully locking the door behind her, and charged down the staircase and through the lobby, wondering where she and Hal were going. She hoped it didn't require taking the subway. The King's Cross underground was busy at night and often filled with disagreeable types. Drunks. Homeless people asking for spare change. People talking nonsense, out of their heads with mental illness or drugs. Or both. Kate took a deep breath and pulled open the door to the street. She could certainly do without King's Cross tonight.

6
William

In the soft light of evening, William again strode toward the garden shed. Above him, the clouds hung soft as wool, a shade darker than the rest of the sky. Black sheep, he thought, and smiled. Some people thought that black sheep were a mark of the devil, which was nonsense. Under all that wool, they were just the same jaunty creatures as the rest of the herd. As William reached the gate, he heard footsteps and stopped short. Who would be following him here? He turned quickly so as not to give away the cub's hiding place. Then he manufactured a smile.

"Good evening, Princess Mary," he said, nodding to Mary's nurse, a woman of questionable authority who stood rubbing her hands. "Are you having an enjoyable stroll?"

"I want to find him!" Mary cried. "I want to find him right now!"

For a moment, William thought she was talking about the wolf cub, and his heart thudded wildly in his chest. Discovery by Mary and her nurse would surely mean death to the creature.

"But Princess Mary, it's past your bedtime," chided the nurse. "Save playing for the morrow."

"I don't want to wait until the morning. I want to play, now! My brother promised to play mumchance with me today and he should keep his word! I wish that cunning woman would give me a ring and I'd make him come to me."

"We should be starting back ..." faltered the nurse as relief swept over William. They had no idea of the hidden animal close at hand.

"Doesn't anyone know where that bad boy is?" Mary asked. William's mouth twitched to hear her refer to her older brother in these terms. To Mary, the Duke of York was merely an irritating sibling, not the royal prince next in line as king. When William did not answer, Mary asked, "Cat got your tongue?" and looked at him slyly.

"Hush," said the nurse. "No need to talk of sorcery, Mary."

"I'm sure Prince Henry didn't mean to break his promise, wherever he is," said William.

"Everyone talks about sorcery!" said Mary. "That cunning woman they caught in the village is going to say who stole the communion cloth. And then they might catch the thief. Or they might hang him. Do you suppose I'll be allowed to see, if they hang that thief until he is dead as a doornail?

William smiled at this phrase and then felt his stomach lurch. How cruel it was to watch people die. He had become so used to the traditions of nobility in these few short months that for a moment he had forgotten his true feelings.

"And I wonder if the communion cloth will ever be found," Mary prattled on. "It was a pretty one, with lots of 'broidery on it."

"Embroidery," corrected the nurse.

"Look," said William, trying make his voice sound inviting, "I'll walk you back to the hall. Maybe there'll be some sugared almonds left from dinner."

"Well ... do you think so?" responded Mary, reluctant but hopeful. "Do you really think there'll be some?"

"I don't know, but we can go and see. I'll race you!" William called, catching the grateful eye of the nurse and then running ahead, but slowly, to give the child a chance to catch up.

"And the prize will be a story!" she cried, passing him. "Last one has to—" here she stopped to breathe heavily "—to tell me a story!"

There were sugared almonds, and Mary took quite a large handful, thought William, looking at the nurse whose attention was taken by one of the menservants asking about her day off. Everyone's affairs were so public here in court, and William blushed to hear the flirtation of a woman old enough to be his mother. Not that she didn't have a right to tend to her relationships. It was just that he preferred not to hear about them.

"And now the story!" said Mary, curling her legs up under herself on the hard bench.

I'd rather fall in a ditch and be bowled with cabbages, thought William. This could take all night, as Mary always had questions that elongated every tale most painfully.

"Very well," he said, in the most cheerful manner he could muster. "What would you like the story to be about?"

"One of your brothers or sisters. Tell a funny story about something bad that happened to them!"

William nodded. Mary always wanted stories about his family. It seemed as if the little girl was trying to make up for her own lack of siblings, with Margaret away in Scotland and Henry busy in his position as Prince Regent.

"Well, there's the tale of Charlotte and the Shoes," he began.

"Is it going to be a funny story?" Mary interrupted.

"Yes, there are funny parts in it."

"And it's serious, too," said Mary. "Make sure it's going to have something bad in it."

"Absolutely, there is a difficult situation here for Charlotte," said William, patiently.

"Go on, then," said Mary. She had the same demanding tone as Prince Henry, but in a child her age, it was rather comical. William suppressed a smile, and began.

"This story is about how Charlotte does not reckon Frank Hopkin among her friends, as she loves him not since the day when he left her in the mud."

"In mud?" interrupted Mary. "Is this the serious part?"

"Yes, Princess," said William. "But let me tell it through, if you please, or I might miss something."

She nodded at him to go on, and he did.

"It was a few years past, when Charlotte was a small maid of eight years and Frank Hopkin was a great lad of thirteen."

"Charlotte is eleven now, so that means it was exactly three years ago!" said Mary triumphantly.

"Yes," said William. "We had gone blackberrying with the Hopkin family, they being neighbors, and Frank, like the imp he was, led the girls home a long way around, and through some thick, dark mud. His sisters made out all right, but Charlotte's shoes did stick, and, being stronger than her, the mud pulled the shoes from off her feet."

Mary laughed and then reconsidered. "But this is a serious part, too," she said.

"Yes," agreed William. "The mud wrestled the shoes from off her feet so that she wept to think of what Mother might say."

"Did your mother scold about things like that?"

"She did, and still does," said William, and then saw a shadow pass over Mary's brow at the thought of having a living mother who cared about what you did. He pressed on.

"The Hopkin girls did manage to avoid the mud, but poor Charlotte floundered in stocking feet, again stuck fast, her shoes by now some distance away. Frank Hopkin stayed to laugh at her a while, and then did kick up his heels and run for home so that his own made-up story might arrive in his defense, before the story his sisters would tell.

"Charlotte screamed and roared but it was of no effect. She was left sticking in the wet mud until word came to me, and I ran to find her in this woeful plight. She had pulled off her stockings, being that they were the second thing stuck after her shoes, and now she stood ankle deep with mud fastening her *bare feet* to the place she stood."

"Oooh!" said Mary. "And did she get a whipping?"

"She did not," replied William. "I informed Mother that it was ill of Frank Hopkin to leave her thus, as he was elder and should be of better constitution."

"And what about Frank Hopkin?" demanded Mary.

"Charlotte decided that he would never be her true love, and so I think he was punished enough," said William, smiling.

"Quite right," said Mary. "I would never grace Frank Hopkin with my attentions, even if he were of royal blood."

"Very wise, Princess," said William. He turned to escape but Mary danced in front of him.

"That was a good story!" she cried. "Another!"

“We’d best leave the storytelling until the morrow,” said William, looking at the nurse who had apparently come to collect her charge. “The sun is quite finished with us and it will soon be time for bed.”

“I hate bed,” said Mary, and the nurse took her hands to lead her away. “See you tomorrow, William!” she called. “I hope you have another story about that Frank Hopkin. He is my favorite of all the ill, naughty, evil, and abominable imps I have heard of lately. I marvel much that he was not at all repentant!”

“Perhaps someday he will mend his ways,” replied William.

“But not very soon!” said Mary. “There are other stories about him, are there not?”

“I believe so,” said William, feeling a bit weary at the thought. “I shall have to think on it.” It struck him that if someone were to create a book of such stories, it might keep Mary satisfied for a good long time, where she could read and reread to her heart’s content. It would be a book for enjoyment, not for learning, and although he had some thought of writing an epistle about farming someday, with collected letters to farmers that advised on modern agricultural techniques, he had never considered any other kind of writing, or its value. *Something to think on,* he repeated to himself. *Definitely something to think on.*

7
The shadows

Kate waited for five minutes in the cool blue shadows of London House and then, miraculously, Hal was there.

"I like a girl who's on time," he said, grinning at her and draping an arm around her shoulders.

"Should I say hello to your sister before we go?"

"She's already gone to the theater," replied Kate.

A flicker of something that looked like disappointment crossed his face.

"All right, then. Let's go," he said. "I can always meet her next time."

Next time! That meant he wanted another date with her! As long as she didn't ruin it. As long as she didn't open her mouth and say something really stupid. As Hal began to walk faster, Kate stepped away. It was difficult keeping up in such close proximity.

"Where ... uh ... where are we going?" Kate asked tentatively.

"You'll see. It'll be fun," Hal said, striding quickly down the path toward Coram's Fields. Kate had to run to catch up. She wished she knew where they were headed.

"What's in there?" she asked, noticing his leather pack.

"A surprise," he said. "For later."

A twinge of irritation added to her unease. She was not a person who liked surprises. When she realized they were bound for the Russell Square tube station, she stopped abruptly. It was one of the undergrounds equipped with an elevator. A very small, airless elevator that Kate had only been in once before and swore she'd never enter again. Hal, already in the doorway of the station, turned to see what was the matter.

"I don't actually like this Underground," she blurted, panic welling up in her chest.

"Really?" he asked. "I'd think a New Yorker like you would be seasoned on the tube. You Americans call them subways, right?"

"Yeah," she said. "This elevator's been stuck loads of times. I read about it in the paper."

"Well, it'll be a long walk," he said a bit briskly, "if you're on foot."

She felt her face grow hot with embarrassment. Why did she have to be such a loser? He must think that she was weird to be okay with one subway but not another. It was just that at King's Cross there were stairs.

"Okay," she mumbled, her face hot with embarrassment. "I'll try it."

"Let's go, then," he said, and she took a deep breath. Self-loathing sloshed around in her stomach. Why did she have to be such a freak? She took another gulp of air and followed him inside the station. A grimy path on the tile floor led them to the lift. It was a small, squalid-looking contraption, hardly big enough to hold the dozen people that were crowding into it.

"We could just take the stairs ..." Kate suggested hopefully, seeing a sign on a nearby door.

"You want to go down a hundred stairs? Be my guest!" Hal snorted. "It wouldn't be my choice. Look," he went on, "I've taken this lift a million times. It's perfectly safe and we'll be out before you know it." He got in boldly, as if to prove his point. Kate moved reluctantly beside him. For a moment, she felt her heart beating harder, her pulse racing, and then, just as Hal had promised, the ride was over.

As they stood on the platform waiting for the train, Kate tried not to think of how far underground they were. The oily smell of the subway made her throat feel sticky, and in the dim light, she could see the tunnel stretching ahead like a tomb. She took a deep breath, just to make sure she still could, and suddenly the car accident in New York rose up in her mind. There had been this terrible noise, and then she'd been crushed in on herself, her breath a sharp exclamation mark in her chest, the car door crumpled and squeezing against her side. Amazing that she hadn't been hurt. When her dad had been ... had been killed. How hard it was to remember this.

"Dad!" she'd yelled, but her father didn't answer. Couldn't answer. And caught in the seat belt, amidst the compacted metal, she hadn't done anything to help. It was all she could do to stay conscious and yell for someone to come and get them out. Except that she was the only one left in the car. He'd been thrown through the front windshield, and when the fire department finally arrived, with the ambulance, it was too late. He was dead.

"Penny for your thoughts?" asked Hal over the rumble of the approaching train. She shook her head, her body beginning to tremble. Caught in the broken car, she'd been sure she'd run out of air, miraculously continuing to breathe until the jaws of life opened a space for the paramedics to get her out. Hal squeezed her hand. Suddenly she caught a glimpse of something plunging along the rails away from them.

"There!" she gasped, the sudden intake of air putting her involuntary shaking to rest. All in a flash, the train was in front of them and Hal was pulling her through the open doorway. What had she seen? Just shadows, or flesh and blood? For a moment, she had been sure she had spotted a wolf.

The train lurched forward and Kate blinked, the view from the scratched window too blurred to see anything. And then they were inside the darkness of the tunnel, and Kate, feeling sick to her stomach, looked away from the glass. The two girls behind them had just finished doing their nails, and the smell of polish stung Kate's nostrils. Nothing like a strong scent to ground you in reality. It must have been shadows she'd seen on the tracks; nothing could live in the underground.

Hal, apparently unconcerned that she hadn't answered his question, was taking gum out of his backpack. The people in the car with them seemed oblivious to anything extraordinary outside. Everyone was busy with something. The guy in front was reading a paperback. Kate craned her neck. It was *Gone with the Wind*. The older man beside him was scanning *The London Times*. Across the aisle, a Goth was gently tugging at a ring embedded in his upper lip, deeply engaged in conversation with the well-dressed businessman beside him. Their banter, reaching Kate's ears, sounded comfortable, warm. They leaned toward each other, obviously partners. How different from each other they look, thought Kate, yet how compatible. She longed for just such an easy relationship, one where communication was effortless. If she wasn't such a loser, maybe she could think of something interesting to say to Hal. She clenched her hands, willing something smart to come out of her mouth, but all she could think of was stuff about the weather, and how dumb was that?

Maybe it hadn't been a wolf back there, she thought. Maybe it was just a dog, a stray who'd somehow found its way down into the tube station. It would run along the tracks and then escape into a side passage at the sound of the approaching train. Or be crushed by the vehicle, its body never found because rats would make swift work of the carcass.

"Come on, it won't kill you," said Hal.

"What?" Kate asked.

Hal waved the gum under her nose. "Gum?"

"Oh, thanks," Kate replied, but she made no move to take any.

"What are you so serious about?" Hal asked.

"Oh ... I ... uh ... was just thinking about our field trip today," she replied with a false laugh, taking the package. "We went to the museum at Greenwich." She popped a piece of gum into her mouth and chewed, the strong smell of mint reminding her of the scene in the forest. She saw again the people on horseback, heard the sound of the hunting horn.

"Ah, the home of time," said Hal. "What did you think of the Prime Meridian?"

"What?" asked Kate, thinking he was talking about numbers.

"The place where all the clocks in the world are set. Zero degrees longitude. You can actually stand with one foot in the eastern hemisphere and one foot in the western hemisphere."

"Well ... I don't think we went there," said Kate, returning the pack of gum.

"Pity," said Hal. "It's a hoot. I've been there loads of times."

"Can you ... can you feel the difference? Between time zones?" asked Kate, her pulse starting to race again.

"You bet," he said. "Sometimes I can almost feel myself disappearing."

"What?" Kate said, startled.

"You can't be in two time zones at the same time, now, can you?" he went on in a light voice. "Sometimes, when you have a choice, you have to pick one time or the other, and then take the consequences."

"You mean change times?" she asked. He gave a short explosive laugh.

"Hah! Well, that's the question, isn't it? The question that people have asked for centuries. Is time travel possible?" She saw all at once that he was joking and tried to smile. When he offered her another piece of gum, she took it and chewed hard, biting her tongue and then blinking as tears came to her eyes.

8
The concert

When they got off the train at Hyde Park Corner, Kate and Hal took the stairs two at a time, bursting out into the mild air. No frost tonight. Still, it was damp, and the hint of cold managed to find its way under Kate's skin.

"Was it that different, then, from your subways?" Hal asked.

Kate paused. For certain, there were no wolves in the New York subways. "No, not much different," she said, finally, "not really," and did her best to smile. She opened her mouth to try the giggle, but nothing came out. Just as well, she told herself. It would likely have been another one of those squeaks. Not very impressive. She wished desperately that she had something interesting to say to Hal, something that would make him laugh or look at her admiringly. Instead, she felt as heavy as a boiled egg, and just as talkative. *Hump-*

ty Dumpty, she thought dismally.

They walked along toward a small crowd that had gathered around a man in striped pants, standing on an apple crate and gesturing wildly. Kate hung back as they approached but Hal pulled her forward.

"These people are a disgrace," said Hal, flinging his arm around Kate's shoulders. "Going to the dogs, that's what's happening to this city."

"I was fell sure I'd had them aw," the man was whining, his voice raspy, his arms outstretched. "But bad omens in these times has brought back the creeshie devils." He cast a bloodshot eye on the handful of onlookers. The way he moved his head reminded Kate of a rusty signboard swinging back and forth, back and forth in the wind.

"Afore ye knows what befell ye—" he continued.

"Okay, move along, move along." A policeman, a *bobby*, Kate thought, had appeared, dispersing the crowd. "Away, or I'll arrest you for disturbing the peace," the bobby said. In response, the small man shook his head from side to side as he backed away, muttering, "They wouldnae listen ... nae, they wouldnae listen ..."

Kate felt a shiver run down her spine. He was creepy. She wondered if he were one of the many homeless people who slept outside. She'd seen the shelters made from cardboard and old quilts. She shivered again, watching him skulk off into the shadows.

"What was that guy talking about?" she asked Hal.

"Wolves," said Hal, snorting, giving her shoulder a squeeze before dropping his arm. "He thinks that London's actually going to the wolves! Says there's a pack here that needs to be hunted down. I heard him last Sunday. 'Course he's cracked in the head."

"But I think ... I think there are wolves here," Kate suddenly confided. "I've ... I think I've seen them, too."

"You must be off your nut!" said Hal. "There haven't been wolves here for hundreds of years. We exterminated them, you know, in about the fifteenth century. Good thing, too, bloodthirsty devils."

A majestic black woman in a sweeping polka-dot muumuu stepped over to them.

"I bet you are wondering," she intoned, "about the power of love."

"No, we're not, actually," snapped Hal in a voice Kate hadn't heard from him before. The woman looked affronted. He doesn't have to speak so roughly, Kate thought.

"For just two pounds, you could share your love with those who need it most," the woman told them.

"Who? Who needs it most?" asked Hal boldly.

"The little children," she answered.

"We don't have time for this," muttered Hal, taking Kate's arm. The smell of something metallic, maybe his deodorant, made Kate take a step away and break free of him.

one else in the building had heard the noise.

She slowly got ready for bed and, as she was brushing her hair, she heard the sound again, not disconnected, as it had been before, but in a series of howls. She went to the window and stared down into the misty street. The eerie cadences rose and fell. Dogs? No. It had to be wolves. A shiver ran down her spine. Something wasn't right, and she thought about phoning Gran again but looked at the clock. Almost midnight. Way too late to call. The howling stopped. She'd phone in the morning. After she had a good sleep to clear her head.

But a good sleep was far from what she had. She dreamed of the tunnel at Greenwich, entering it in the company of a great gray wolf with steely eyes. The wolf seemed to be her guide, and she moved alongside it with some anxiety, making sure not to get too close. There was something the wolf was searching for, something it wanted her to find. What could it be? And then, without satisfying her curiosity, she awoke, sweating in tightly bound covers, relieved at being able to breathe again but dismayed at the puzzles the dream had conjured.

Awake in the dark, her mind spun to the animal she'd seen in the Underground. And the crazy man in Hyde Park, talking about bad omens. For a moment, Kate wondered if she had dreamed the date, dreamed, in fact, the whole day. But when she thought of Hal's kiss, she knew it had been real, his lips against hers. The memory of that kiss distracted her until the sound of a door slamming separated Kate from her thoughts. The hall light came on and, in an instant, Willow was in Kate's bedroom doorway, looking furious.

"Why didn't you lock the door before you went to bed!" she said. "You know we've always got to keep the flat locked!"

"I guess I forgot," Kate mumbled.

"You're just too lazy to think about safety!" yelled Willow. "Why don't you just grow up!"

She turned and slammed the door behind her.

"Okay, be that way, Miss Perfect," muttered Kate.

Sleep didn't come for a long time after that, and when it did, there were no more dreams. When Kate awoke, it was Saturday morning, and the blue dress was stretched across the foot of her bed.

9
The dress

Kate reached out for the dress just as Willow called, "Wake up, sleepyhead! Have a look at your early birthday present." Her voice held no trace of last night's anger.

"The dress? It's for me?" Kate asked sleepily.

"Don't act innocent," Willow answered. "I know you already found it in my closet! Anyway, since you've already seen it, I thought I'd get you to try it on. Then I'll finish that side seam so it'll be ready for Monday, the big day. You might want to wear it to school or something."

The idea of wearing this dress to school on her fifteenth birthday made Kate roll her eyes, but she said, "Wow! Uh ... maybe." Might as well humor her sister.

"It was extra from the show," said Willow, stretching out her long, model's legs to sit on the side of Kate's bed and running a hand through her short blonde hair. "The costume mistress made it for Katherine of Aragon—you know, Henry VIII's first wife. And then the director didn't like the blue. He wanted cornflower blue, not gentian blue, or something like that. Anyway, this one wouldn't do, so Ariana offered it to anybody for cheap. I thought you might like it. Your wardrobe could use a lift. You wear such ugly stuff."

"It's not like I want to wear that stupid uniform," Kate said defiantly, sitting up and swinging her legs out of bed. Next to Willow's, they looked short and plump.

"Well, it's for after school, then," said Willow, smoothing the fabric of her own stylish top where it wrinkled above the waistband of her tight jeans. "Don't get huffy. You must get tired of sweatshirts."

"Not really," Kate began, conscious of the gray sweatshirt she'd slept in. It was easier to sleep in your clothes than change, and she did it quite often.

"Live a little!" advised Willow. "And for goodness sakes, *do something* today other than hanging around. Run, walk, anything! You always used to run back home, and I think it kept you from being so melancholy. Now, try on the dress and I'll finish that seam."

"I'm not melancholy and I did try it on," Kate said. "Before. And it's too tight."

Willow grinned triumphantly. "I knew it! Sneak!"

Kate scowled.

"It's a Tudor dress," said Willow. "Straight from the history book." She held the dress against Kate to check the size. "You'll be the envy of everybody if you wear this to the play on Wednesday night. That's Preview Night, don't forget!" She looked at her sister thoughtfully. "You've got the figure for this style, unlike me. I'm way too flat for this neckline."

Kate looked down at herself. Flat was not a word she would have used to describe what she saw.

"And the color will look good on you," Willow continued. "Blue always looks nice on redheads."

Big Apple, Kate remembered, and flushed.

"The Tudor period was a fine one for dresses," Willow said, stopping for a breath and then going on. She'd make a good tour guide, thought Kate, with her foghorn voice. "You can see bits of the same style returning now, all the way from the 1500s. The square necklines, for example. You know, the walls between worlds are thinner than you'd think."

"What?" said Kate, startled.

"You know, styles and fashion, moving from one time into another," Willow went on. "Hurry up and get out of bed. You've got to come and help me with something before I leave. Robert wants to go through a couple of scenes today and I need you to run some lines. Help me with some back story for my reactions to Katherine. There's soup for brunch."

"Ooh, *Robert,*" said Kate. "Will it be just you and him all by yourselves?" Willow didn't answer.

"What kind of soup?" Kate asked with some misgiving as she headed to the shower.

"A new kind," said Willow, a hint of pride in her voice. "I

mixed split pea with cream of cabbage. It's really good."

Kate groaned and turned on the water as she heard the sound of the sewing machine. "Make the dress a lot wider!" she called. "So I can breathe!"

When Kate came out of the bathroom, Willow had already put away the sewing machine and was paging through her script. Kate hated running lines with her sister, and this play—*Henry VIII*—was particularly hard. Shakespeare's language was so confusing, and Willow always stopped and explained things until Kate felt as if her head was going to explode. She'd much rather get out her math book and solve equations. At least with math, it was clear when you were done. She heaved a deep sigh and plopped down beside her sister.

"Read from there," Willow indicated. "Scene four, where Queen Katherine of Aragon is supposed to be speaking up for herself after King Henry has denounced their marriage as unlawful. Basically, he's got the hots for Anne Boleyn, that's me, and he's been trying to find a way to annul his first marriage. In Tudor times, divorce wasn't permitted. Robert says ..." her voice droned on as Kate reluctantly eyed the text. Katherine's speech looked really long.

"That's twice today you've mentioned Robert," interrupted Kate, trying to distract her sister from the task at hand. "Is he cute?"

"Don't be silly," snapped Willow. "He's Canadian. From

Quebec. An amazing director. And he's too old for me. Okay, we don't have a lot of time—start reading. I need to determine my reactions to Katherine, and listening to this speech will help."

"Age doesn't matter when you're really in love!" said Kate.

"Just start!" commanded Willow.

Kate began to read aloud. After a few lines, Willow stopped to paraphrase.

"So Katherine's saying that Henry should stay married to her out of pity because she's a foreigner and also that he should admire her because she's always been true to him."

"Oh," said Kate. "What about love? If he doesn't love her, maybe it's better he goes for this Anne Bowling."

"Boleyn! My character's name is Anne Boleyn, rhyming with *pin*, as in *Pinhead*!" Willow rattled on about Anne Boleyn, but Kate was thinking about their neighbor.

"You never see Martin Brown with his wife," Kate blurted. "I wonder why that is. Maybe they're divorced. First I thought he reminded me of a raven but, really, he's more like a blackbird with that shiny dark hair."

"We're talking about the early 1500s," Willow snapped, "when the church was very strict about marriage and there was no such thing as divorce if you were a Catholic."

"So that's why Henry killed some of his wives?" Kate asked. "Because he couldn't divorce them? Why didn't he kill Katherine?"

"Their marriage was dissolved," replied Willow. "Because Katherine had first been married to Henry's brother who died. *King Henry the eighth to six wives he was wedded: one died, one survived, two divorced, two beheaded,*" Willow quipped.

"What happens to you in the end?" asked Kate. "To Anne?"

"I get beheaded," said Willow smugly. "For treason. They accuse me of taking other lovers."

"And Katherine?" Kate asked, flipping through the script.

"She dies from cancer of the heart, if you can believe that. But she signs her name Katherine the Queen until the end."

"Out of stubbornness?" asked Kate.

"Maybe. Or love," said her sister. "Now, read me that whole speech again. Where Katherine's trying to convince Henry not to leave her."

"Do I have to?"

"Yes."

Kate sighed. It felt as if they had worked long enough, but she couldn't argue with her stubborn sister. She wished again that they were doing math. They bent their heads over the script until Willow finally jumped up, looking at her watch. "Gotta go," she said.

"Why was she called Katherine of Aragon?" asked Kate.

"She was the daughter of a Spanish king," said Willow.

"Oh," said Kate. "So if Dad had been a king, we'd be Willow and Kate of New York."

"Yeah, I guess," said Willow, stuffing some things into a bag. "But you act snobby enough without having any royal blood."

"I do not!" said Kate, anger flaring.

"You do. Have you even tried to make friends here?" Willow looked at her sharply.

"I know lots of people," retorted Kate.

"Who? Name somebody from school!"

"Well, Naomi!" yelled Kate, offering the first name that came to mind. Naomi had once asked Kate to join the school newspaper. That counted as friendship, didn't it? And Amandella seemed as if she'd like a friend.

"So, ask Naomi to Preview Night," said Willow. "Ask anyone you like. There'll be lots of extra tickets. And why don't you go visit Gran today?" Willow's voice became even more amplified until Kate longed for the *off* button. "You could take the train and be back before bedtime. Do her some good."

"I'm busy today," snapped Kate.

"Doing what?" bellowed Willow. "What are you so busy doing?"

"Well ... homework," said Kate defiantly.

"Okay, well, that's good," responded Willow a little more quietly and then picking up volume along with speed. "But you should really go up and see Gran sometime, okay? I'll be tied up for the next few weekends with the run of the show.

But you should go up there. She gets lonely. And try on the dress, would you, to make sure it fits? I'll stay and grab a bite at the theater if we run late this afternoon. Now make sure you eat the—"

"Soup. I know!" Kate groaned, interrupting her sister's tirade. "Just shut up, okay? I'm not a baby. I can take care of myself."

"Well, if you're not a baby," said her sister bluntly, "you should stop acting like one. When was the last time you cleaned up around here or did anything, in any way, to help out?"

"Who died and made you King?" snapped Kate and then suddenly realized what she'd said. As a deep flush spread across her face, Willow went out of the room as if she hadn't heard, but Kate knew they both had caught the unintended reference to their father and their current circumstances.

"I'll leave the soup on the cooker, on *low*, so don't forget," Willow called from the kitchen.

"Why do you call it a *cooker*?" said Kate nastily to cover up her own embarrassment. "Seems like we always used to call it a *stove* before. Are you trying to pretend you're British?"

Willow didn't answer.

"I bet you're trying to convince people here that you are a real Brit," Kate said. "Actresses are so good at pretending."

10
Disappearing

Kate finished a little soup and a piece of toast and then licked the butter from her fingers before heading to her room to try on the dress. The light beside her bed had made the room hot and so she flipped the switch before draping the blue gown across the quilt and removing her sweatshirt. As she eased the silky fabric over her head, she felt the same panicky feeling as before, and although the dress slid down easily over her jeans without being tight, she felt her breath catch in her throat. Then it was on and she looked in the mirror. The dress did look nice. She turned sideways. Very nice, in fact. She wished Hal were there to see her. What had Willow said? *Live a little.*

A sudden odor of burnt soup sent her racing to the kitchen, where the remains of the nasty concoction sizzled in the pot. She'd forgotten to turn off the burner. By the time she had finished cleaning up, Kate's arms ached from scrubbing. She wished she could just throw away the pot with the rest of the garbage, but it was their only one. After it was as clean as possible, she decided she'd better get rid of the burnt remains that were stinking up the kitchen, so she headed out with the garbage bag to the rubbish bin at the back of the building.

Stopping for a moment in the hall, she thought about returning to change her clothes, but then gave in to the moment. *Live a little.* She could go outside in this outfit just as well as in anything else. And sweeping about in this fairy creation did feel nice. She practically flew down the stairs and out the door, and then whirled elegantly as she heaved the bag into the trash can, enjoying the sensation of the fabric billowing out around her. Unexpected voices made her scurry behind the sheltering bins, peering out to see who was coming. Two people walked side by side toward the old cemetery that stretched out behind the lane, and one of them looked oddly familiar. She took a small step closer where she could get a better look. It was Hal. Walking with him was a girl of about Kate's age, with long blonde hair swept back in a French braid. The girl was petite—probably no more than a hundred pounds, Kate thought—and had a laugh like tinkling bells. With a sinking feeling, Kate wondered if the girl could be Hal's sister. As the girl laughed a second time, Kate saw Hal lean in and kiss her full on the lips. The girl stepped toward him and Kate turned away, a warm flush rising from her neck to her cheeks. The two-timer! Who did he think he was!

She backed further into the shadows, her face on fire. When she saw the two figures turn as if to walk her way, she squirmed over the low stone wall that bordered the alley and began to run. The last thing she wanted was for the two of them to find her mincing around in this costume. She soon got the hang of running in the flowing skirt, and as long as she held it well above her ankles, it caused no difficulty.

She headed along Guilford Street and when a double-decker bus stopped in front of her, she got on. There was an awkward moment when she hiked up her dress to retrieve the money she had in her jeans, but she quickly handed over the fare and then dropped stiffly down onto a leather seat. She didn't know where the bus was going and she didn't care. She just wanted to get as far away as she could.

After a few blocks of travel, possibilities began to creep into her mind. Perhaps she'd been mistaken. Maybe Hal was still making up his mind about who he really liked. Maybe he wasn't exactly her boyfriend, not yet, but maybe he could be. Maybe he'd tried to call her but since he didn't have her number, he'd gone out with this other girl, who, from what Kate had seen, was pretty pushy. Maybe Kate would just see how things went the next time Hal asked her out.

Kate realized that her throat felt raw and she could taste

blood in her mouth. It had been a long time since she'd run like that. Too long. The beginning of a nosebleed sent her off the bus and into a tube station washroom, hunting for paper towels.

"Serves me right," she thought, "for not staying in shape."

As she left the tube station, her nose aching into her forehead, she noticed a sign with directions to Greenwich Park. She headed that way, crossing a bridge and then wandering through the streets, admiring the architecture of the buildings. She thought hazily of going to the Prime Meridian that Hal had talked about. The home of time. Might as well explore a bit, she decided. The weather was fair and she had nothing else to do.

The village of Greenwich, now considered part of London, boasted Tudor inns among Georgian and Victorian cottages, the mix of architectural styles intriguing. As if in a daze, Kate walked through the town center, up Nevada Street, and through St. Mary's gate into Greenwich Park. As a misty rain began to fall, she headed instinctively toward the Thames and soon found herself once again walking beside the landlocked *Cutty Sark,* her feet stumbling along the trail she had taken the previous day.

I wish I could just disappear, she thought, shivering slightly, the familiar phrase beating a tattoo in her brain. *Disappear and never have to worry about anything again.* Her eye caught the knowing gaze of the figurehead of the ship, thinking that it looked both shrewd and compassionate. "What are you looking at!" she muttered as she passed, imagining its gaze boring into her back.

Rain began in earnest and she stepped quickly off the path and into the dry air of the same tunnel she'd been in yesterday. There was a strange throbbing at the back of her head and her hands and feet tingled. Turning toward the entrance, she was astounded to see a mirror image of herself—a girl in a long blue dress—and then realized it was another girl, the girl she'd seen in the clearing in that other world. Their eyes met and a current of something—electricity?— flashed between them. Suddenly drawn away from the girl, Kate tumbled to her knees, listening to the sound of her own captive heart as the world was once more rushing by. "Wait!" called Kate, her voice echoing in her ears. She was again swept headily into darkness, yet instead of the flat absence of being, this time, pictures filled her mind, foreign images that somehow seemed familiar.

First there were scenes of apple trees and flower gardens; then a tall black carriage, drawn by a dozen black horses; she next fancied herself standing at a door that she wanted to open, and yet, at the same time, a door she wished would stay shut. It was a large wooden door, ornately carved, with a huge brass doorknob. Someone was behind that door who would make a pronouncement that could change her life, if only he would. But he couldn't be rushed. She must stand

and wait. And pray. Abruptly jarred back to the reality of the tunnel, Kate tried to stand up, but the pressure against her was too great and she fell back in a heap, black spots darting in front of her eyes. She seemed to be sweeping toward a crossroads where the tunnel divided left and right. Instinctively, she leaned her body to the right, and then everything went dark.

When she came to her senses, she was sitting on a rocky knoll a few feet from the tunnel's opening. Shakily, she brushed the prickly dust from her ankles, then stood and stumbled into the same clearing she'd discovered yesterday. A hissing sound came from overhead and when she looked carefully, she saw a small gray and brown woodpecker perched on a branch, regarding her with beady eyes. The hissing sound came from its beak. The bird reminded her of an old woman trying to cast some kind of spell.

A wryneck, she thought with sudden assurance, surprised that she was able to identify it, for she'd never in her life seen one. Had she read about them? She wasn't sure.

"I'm not dreaming," she said to the sharp-eyed bird, its shrewd gaze somehow familiar. "I'm not."

As if in answer, the bird stopped its ruckus and cocked its head.

"That's better," she announced. "For a minute, I thought you were trying to put a curse on me." The bird stretched its wings and flew away.

What am I doing here? thought Kate, trying to get her balance and inhaling the now familiar smell of mint. She wished she hadn't entered the tunnel a second time. *What was I thinking?* she asked herself. A law she remembered from physics class entered her thoughts: *Everything seeks the path of the most disorder.* But that wasn't true. She wanted order. She wanted desperately to explain things in a way that made sense, but here she was, with no more answers than before. Something caught her eye in the woods and, with immediate revulsion, she realized that a dead deer was hanging from a nearby branch, supported upside down with ropes around its pelvis.

It's there to age, she thought with unusual clarity, so that the meat grows more tender. How did she know this? No one she knew had ever hunted. The dizzy feeling returned. Suddenly, crackling branches caught her attention. Before she could step back to hide, a black horse plunged through the underbrush, its rider guiding it skillfully among the trees and, at the same time, leading a dappled gray pony. It was the same red-haired fellow she'd seen yesterday, only this time his gaze fell directly on her. She instinctively tried to duck behind some of the larger tree trunks, but her skirt caught in brambles and she was pinned like a butterfly until the rider approached.

"The game is up!" he said, slipping from the saddle to stand not more than a few inches away. "How you have changed, Katherine. Your hair—it is cut?"

"The game?" Kate repeated numbly, staring into his kingfisher blue eyes. She struggled to loosen the cloth of her skirt, overwhelmed with the sensation that she knew this person. Knew him well.

"Our little hide and seek. My party has now returned to the castle, and perhaps it is not too much to expect that you will tell me what you are doing here? I would warrant I deserve an answer."

The formality of his speech startled Kate, and she stood staring, incapable of a response.

"Has the cat got your tongue?" he asked. "No, never mind. I only jest."

Although his words were confusing, Kate interpreted the flashing in his blue eyes as teasing, not anger. His gleaming hair was combed straight down over his forehead, accentuating his striking eyes and strong features. He had what Gran would call a noble brow.

"We will ride back together. Are you able to mount?" he asked.

The gray pony had trotted alongside Kate and she automatically lifted herself into the sidesaddle, aware that this knowledge of practice was not—could not—be her own. Somehow in transit, perhaps in connection with that other girl, she had collected information that was now coming in handy.

"Your horse will follow mine, as always," he said.

She did not respond, her head throbbing wildly with the inflated sense that she was more than one person.

"You have an unusual way of offering surprises," he called back to her moments later. "I did not expect to see you return just yet."

"I didn't—" Kate began, and then another, more formal voice took over in response to the young man's cadences: "Of course, I did not—" but here she stopped herself. A memory of riding hard through autumn fields snapped into her mind and she couldn't brush it away. As in the tunnel, when she thought of the black carriage, the shut door, and even in her skill at riding, foreign memories overpowered her.

"Of course you will have to tell me sooner or later, but if you prefer to wait, I must be patient," he said, gracefully guiding his stallion through the trees. "Although the royal palace is close by, I do have one important errand before I return, and you will accompany me."

The royal palace? Kate glimpsed a turret in the distance, as well as blue water, and then these images were obscured by branches as the horses moved ahead, her mount following his. What was this place?

Kate sat back as best she could and clutched the saddle, holding on more tightly as they found the path and the horses began to gallop. Her hands grew numb and she tried to relax her grip, but it was impossible under the circumstances. Her position on the horse was comfortable, but her mind was alert to danger, sure at any moment that she'd go tumbling to the ground. Soon they reached a clearing and the horses slowed and came to a halt, the young man sliding from the saddle and then lifting Kate down beside him. He was slightly taller than she, and muscular. He'd lifted her easily. Stepping back, she took full note of what he was wearing—a rich green tunic with brown leggings and narrow leather loafers. It was an odd sort of style that matched his formal way of speaking.

"Just a short stop," he said, indicating a small thatched cottage encircled by a low hedge. "I've got some business here." He tied the reins of both horses to a branch and then strode purposefully up to the house. Kate looked around. She remembered from class that Greenwich Park was quite large—seventy-four hectares, she thought—and home to a small herd of fallow deer. Hunting must be illegal, though. Was she in any danger because of what she had seen? Could he be afraid she'd turn him in as a poacher? A nasty smell hung about the yard, thick and poisonous, and Kate wrinkled her nose. She hesitated, not knowing where to turn. A puppy playing in the grass caught her attention and she took a few steps in its direction.

"MacQueen," called the red-haired fellow authoritatively. "Show yourself."

"You're welcome, sir," came a raspy voice, and then a little man, much shorter than either of them, stepped out of the doorway into the yard, kicking aside two other puppies. He had bushy dark brows over bloodshot green eyes and a sneering expression of delight at seeing his visitors. Except for the pipe he held in the corner of his mouth, he strongly resembled the fellow she'd seen standing on the apple crate in the park. Was he one and the same? She couldn't decide.

She wrinkled her nose. There was a mound of gray skins beside the cottage, ragged and moldy. It looked as though they had been there for years. Behind them, Kate could see a refuse pile, topped with rotten pumpkins and squash, and more skins underneath. No wonder the place smelled rank.

"I've been vigilant but have not seen nary a one," her companion went on. "Shall I let my father the King know that you have completed your task?"

"Indeed, every tenant within the bounds did confirm that the great grays are all gone," whined MacQueen, shuffling a little as he spoke. He seemed to be one of those people who could never look you straight in the eye and so was always moving during a conversation, sidestepping, shifting about, his head tilting first to one side and then the other. *Like a rusty sign, swinging in the wind,* thought Kate. The creepy feeling of déjà vu intensified.

To hide her discomfort, she knelt down to stroke the puppy that was now nipping at the hem of her dress, all the while continuing to study the little man. There was something about MacQueen that looked menacing even though he seemed harmless enough. She wouldn't want to be alone with him.

"And none are left?" asked Kate's companion. His commanding voice made him seem older than his years, but Kate thought he was about her age or perhaps a little younger.

"I'd not say there was," the man whined. "I'd best say they're all gone."

"You're talking in riddles," snapped the young man, lifting his hand as if to strike. "Either they are gone, or they are not!" Kate shivered at his demeanor, the pleasant gallantry of a few minutes ago replaced by fury.

"Well, in the fields and wild places of Scotland, there could be some small plenty of the great grays," MacQueen snuffled, sidling a few steps toward the cottage. "But here, there are nae ones to assail you. I've made sure all are away." He grinned, and repeated in the same whining tone as before: "All are away."

Great grays. Could they be talking about wolves? Was this man MacQueen helping to get rid of wolves? A smug feeling washed over Kate. So she really had seen wolves! And this certainly was the man she'd heard ranting in the park!

"You're hunting wolves," Kate said dizzily, more as a statement than a question.

Her companion looked at her in horror, and MacQueen cried, "Whisht, besom, hush your blether! It's an ill thief that speaks sae bold!" He crossed himself and turned to face the young man as if for affirmation.

The puppy suddenly took a great tug at Kate's hem and she heard fabric ripping.

"Hey, stop that!" she said, trying to release the little teeth but instead gaining a scratch on the hand from the creature's eager claws.

"By St. George, a noble pup!" said her companion, striding over and carefully releasing the animal's paw from her skirt. "He is healthy, then?" he asked MacQueen. Kate wondered if he were trying to change the subject on purpose, to mask some kind of blunder on her part. Surely you were allowed to speak of wolves—there couldn't be a law against that! The world swayed around her and she put out a hand to steady herself.

"The whelps are all fine, your grace, an's their dam," said MacQueen, indicating the mother dog who now lay suckling her other pups in a roughly made bed of straw beside the garden shed.

"Ah, this one's a brave lad, isn't he," said the young man, scratching the puppy around its ears. "A fine son you have," he called out to the mother as he picked up the pup and carried him to be with his siblings. His voice rang out among the trees and echoed back, lifting as if it held an important message. "May you have many strong sons."

"And for yourself the same," whined MacQueen.

"I thank you kindly, sir," replied Kate's companion.

"What kind of dogs are these?" Kate asked in a high thin voice, her stomach lurching from the sweetish smell of decay.

The two stared at her incredulously. After a moment, MacQueen spoke in a sneering sort of way.

"Ho, they'll be His Highness's own wolfhounds, then, Princess Katherine," he said. He looked over at the young man. "I am glad all is settled."

"Nothing is settled unless I say it is so," was the quick reply. Taking a pouch from around his waist, the young man threw it at MacQueen's feet.

Kate looked from one to the other. *MacQueen and the Duke of York, an unlikely pair. Yet Henry's father asked much of him in affairs of home and state. Being heir to the throne was more than just formality—it took a good deal of training.* Kate froze at these thoughts. Where had they come from? MacQueen broke the tension by picking up the pouch and removing one of the items—a dog collar, spiked with silver and gold.

"For the whelps." He nodded at his own words and then added in an ingratiating manner, obviously intent on Henry's favor: "Very good, very good. I wish ye much joy of them." Then he actually bowed before turning and shuffling back inside the cottage. Kate looked again at the skins with the sickening knowledge of their origin. Wolf pelts, oozing in the sun, the flies feasting on the aged, ill-cleaned hides.

Henry, if indeed that was his name, caught up the horses' reins. As he led the animals toward Kate, he carefully looked her over.

"Are you quite well?" he asked, stopping a few paces away.

"Yes. Yes, I'm fine," she said.

"Very good. Because I wouldn't want to chance riding with you if the sweating sickness had returned." He eyed her warily.

"I am quite well," Kate heard herself saying in this other voice that was remarkably hers and yet not hers, a voice whose accents seemed foreign and strange. Was it possible that she could be herself, and yet someone else, at the same time?

He took her left hand and, turning it over, traced a finger along the palm where Kate's scar shone white in the sunlight.

"Yes, yes, very good," Henry said, looking up as she glanced back toward the hut. "Don't let him bother you," he went on, helping her to mount the gray horse. "Soon, Princess Katherine, he'll be returned to Scotland, for his job is nigh done." *Princess Katherine.*

"Oh, but I'm not—" She was about to deny the title when her horse stepped forward and she had to put all her effort into balancing and hanging on. She had ridden a few times before, back in the United States when she and her father drove to a stable for a few hours' ride, but she by no means was an experienced rider, and this saddle required that she sit twisted at the waist, with both legs hanging down on the same side. Yet somehow she adjusted, just as she had done earlier, and in a few minutes her body relaxed, the effort of co-ordinating the ride exchanged for practiced ease. In contrast to her riding stance, her mind burst with discomfort. How could she ride like this? Even without the sidesaddle, she recalled bouncing in all her previous riding attempts, nothing like what she was experiencing today.

I have ridden a great deal, she thought, with the added consciousness of another's voice inside her head. *Practiced the equestrian arts ever since I was a child.* With this thought, she felt herself sliding from the saddle, and the next thing she knew, she was lying in the bushes.

"Wake up!" the young man was calling and she stared at him blankly. "My God, Katherine, wake up! Are you hurt?"

"I am quite well," she said, her voice measured and even. "Please help me to my feet, and we shall finish the journey, but a little slower, if you please. I am weary as I have been traveling a long time this day."

Seated in the saddle again, her mind increased its energy, flitting like a sparrow from one episode to the next until she felt completely worn out. As they rode, the young man kept turning and eyeing her with concern. Who was this guy? He certainly seemed to know her. Conscious of his attention, Kate thought with a jolt of something he had said earlier: *My father the King.*

Who am I? she asked herself, probing the memories that continued to surprise her as she guided the pony along the path behind the black horse. The clothes here, the formality of the language, even the trappings of the horses were bewildering and yet somehow commonplace. Questions flooded her mind about every detail, asking what it all meant and where exactly she was. Then, even more urgently, she muttered to herself, *And when?*

11
William

Brushing the hair out of his eyes, William carefully opened the door to the shed and stepped inside. He smiled as he noticed that the bowl he'd filled yesterday was now empty. That was a good sign.

"Good boy!" he said to the cub, and the animal wriggled a little as if it understood that William was pleased. Pouring the jar of bread and milk into the bowl, William prayed the creature would be strong enough to eat this fare, and his prayers were rewarded.

As William rubbed strong-smelling grease onto the wounded front leg, the cub didn't growl but remained very still until the process was finished. William couldn't deduce the ingredients, for the vessel was from the stables and he did not know what the servants had used, but he recognized the scent from a similar concoction his mother had mixed for the lambs. He'd helped her make lip balm ... and there were some similarities between it and this mixture, although this was definitely more powerful. Nostalgically, he remembered the bottle containing oil of roses his mother always kept in the shadows of the kitchen shelf. Charlotte's job had been to collect the roses each spring, and he remembered her going out with a little basket and coming in proudly, the task completed.

Therein might be another story for Mary, thought William. The story of Charlotte and the roses. How one day, when their mother was making rose water for gooseberry fool, she asked Charlotte to collect some fresh petals. Instead of gathering the wild roses that grew along the lane, Charlotte, thinking to make her task easier, went into Father's garden and pillaged all the robust blooms she could find. When Father returned from the fields and noticed the barren beds, he'd been very angry, thinking the wind had done it. As Charlotte watched him eat his third helping of dessert, heartily giving into his sweet tooth, she'd started to cry, and then finally confessed the whole story.

"What a great hearty hog I am," their father had said, "to eat up my very best roses!" Then he and all the rest of them had laughed together until Charlotte had dried her tears. You could always count on Father to turn a dark situation light. William sighed. Was there anything that gave his father laughter now? Or were his days dark and solemn from morn to night?

After giving the wolf cub's fur a good brushing to prevent the fleas from settling in, William sat back and contemplated the weak little animal. It had eaten well, and that was a good thing. It also seemed to trust him, which would simplify its care. How long until the leg was well, William could not say, but the salve would help. Perhaps in a few days, the creature might be well enough to go back to the woods. Except for the problem of its singular state. Wolves, he knew, live in packs, with the senior animals hunting for the younger ones. How would this little thing fare, all on its own?

William put aside his worries of the future. It would do no good to think too far ahead. If the infection in the leg worsened, going back to the woods wouldn't be a problem, for the animal would not be alive to go anywhere. He slapped at a flea that was tickling the hairs on his arm. Blasted pest. Insects did not deserve the space they occupied in nature! I'd rather be tramped by a dozen sheep than left for the fleas to ingest, he thought, and then jumped as the wolf cub's rough tongue rasped against the back of his hand. He lowered his hand a little further. "Enjoy the salt," he said, and then offered his other hand as well. The cub licked both hands before falling back onto its resting place.

"You'll be all right," William said, standing up and surveying the shed, then turning to the door. "I'll be back after dark," he called over his shoulder, feeling the need to communicate something if only through the sound of his voice. Animals had just as much need of reassurance as people did.

Hope coursed through him at the thought of restoring this little animal to health, just as he would restore his father to freedom, if only he could. It was his father who had taught him to respect the natural world, just as his father had shown compassion for all living things, human or not. For Father, who so loved the out of doors, imprisonment would be devastating. Now, William felt new resolve. This afternoon he would speak again to Prince Henry. Perhaps he could finally persuade his friend to bend the ear of the King on the elder Fitzroy's behalf. His father had not been involved in any kind of treachery, of that William was sure. He was, in fact, a loyal follower of the King, and had only the misfortune of being related by marriage to the nephews of Richard III, poor little lads, who had disappeared from the Tower so many years ago. If there was any plot to locate these nephews and return them to the throne, John Fitzroy was certainly unaware of it.

William quickly stepped out of the garden and then, just as quickly, darted back to retrieve his cloak. As he walked down the path toward the castle, he could hear dogs barking in the distance and shivered, brushing the hair from his eyes. It was the sound of a hunt, and he wondered what the target was this time. Some unlucky animal in the wrong place at the wrong time. As perhaps he himself was, here in court. Everything about courtly life still felt foreign, even though he'd already been here some months. "I'd rather be bowled with giant beets," he said to himself, absently scratching his neck, "than spend another fortnight in Placentia." But in truth, he had little choice in the matter and he knew it.

His mother was a second cousin to Prince Henry's late mother, Elizabeth of York, and so William's connections to the royal family were clear. Henry's grandmother, Margaret Beaufort, had called him here to be one of the Duke's peers in spite of the senior William's disgrace. It was because of his father's imprisonment that William had wanted to come, determined to find a way to clear his father's name. But it felt so hopeless.

Though I should walk in the midst of the shadow of death, I will fear no evils, for thou art with me. Thy rod and thy staff, they have comforted me, thought William. The words of the psalm didn't have the same power as they did when Charlotte said them, but they were familiar. And then something his mother often said came back to him, the words slow and comforting in the face of what seemed like an insurmountable task. *Things are not always what they seem.* He repeated the words to himself now as a kind of promise, and then stopped to listen. The baying of the dogs had stopped.

12
The royal palace

As they rode along through the woods, Kate tried not to show the interior battle that was occurring. Contrasting thoughts pulled her this way and that, and uppermost was the idea that she had to be cautious about what she said and did. If she, a stranger, had witnessed anything illegal, this fellow would be treating her differently. Instead, he seemed to know her well and treated her gently. Although she did not know where she was or where they were going, somehow the terrain was familiar, the direction they took stirring up phrases of distant memory: it won't be long now. We're almost home. Home?

What her mind kept settling on was the idea that she had somehow traveled outside of her London time zone and ended up in a different time altogether. A completely different time. But was that possible? Logic whirled her back to details from books she'd read. According to the laws of physics, time travel was indeed possible if one went faster than the speed of light. The speed of light squared, she remembered.

Of course, travel even at the speed of light wasn't possible, unless one considered tachyon theory. She considered what she knew about tachyons, charged particles that could be attracted to points at the end of each universe. If the tachyons were drawn to the holes at each end of the tunnel, there would be opposing currents, and the particles themselves would be drawn back and forth through the tunnel, creating an unusual force field. Which would explain the shimmering greenish light—a kind of radiation. Such a force field could distort matter to the physical property it would need to shift between worlds.

Hysterical laughter bubbled up as she contemplated the prospect of being carried through time. Not my idea of a holiday vacation, she muttered, looking down at the dust that still coated her bruised ankles. It occurred to her that this dust could be collections of spent tachyons, particles that had lost their charge. If she was indeed in a time long past, then tachyon theory was a plausible explanation. But what had created the tunnels in the first place? Something had carved them out, had needed the passages so desperately that digging toward escape had become supernatural. The entrances, she mused, seemed stable in terms of place, but perhaps the times at either end could fluctuate, depending on the particular journey one took. Kate remembered leaning a little to the right just before things went dark. Maybe this was what had taken her beyond yesterday's arrival.

The young man, Henry, turned again to scrutinize her. "Are you quite all right?" he called. "I can see you shivering."

"Fine," Kate called. "I am quite well." *I have to get a grip on myself,* she thought. It would be so easy to lose control. She stared at the scenery. Nothing, and yet everything, was familiar. The parks she knew in London were not at all like this, and yet she felt she somehow knew this place. She was connected here with a history she couldn't explain. She suddenly recalled other times with Henry—his arms around her, his voice soft against her ear. *But maybe it's all just a dream,* she thought desperately. *It has to be!*

It occurred to her just as suddenly that maybe the present situation was real, and what she remembered from before was a dream. The accident, her father's death, living with her sister—maybe these were the products of her imagination, and real life was what she was currently experiencing. Her mind ached at this possibility, a chance, here at her fingertips, for escape from all that troubled her.

"There!" called Henry as they passed the original hunting site and Kate turned her head from the sight of the dead deer. Instead, she gazed exhaustedly at the marsh and then at the foliage that concealed the mouth of the tunnel. Every pore of her body felt stretched and sore. "Not long now!" he called, glancing back at her with what she interpreted as a worried look. They moved out of the lush woodlands and through a ravaged area of forest, toward an upward-sloping plane. The ground here was reduced to black stubble and the trees stood dark and thin as wires. It looked like a planned burn, its parameters forming what seemed to be a measured quadrant on one side of a grassy hill. What had caused such destruction? Who would burn down an entire forest?

The view from the top of the hill was stunning. At the end of a long stretch of lawn stood the palace. Kate's skin tingled. *My father the King.* Towers and turrets stretched up into the heavens, red brick walls framing a building more massive than any she had seen in New York or London. Most of the structure rose into a second story, but at the far end she could see a tower five stories tall. They passed through stone gates, around which clustered a ragged-looking crowd, men and women holding out their hands beseechingly to the young man while a few scrawny children played in the dirt.

"You shall have your supper," her companion called out to them, throwing over a handful of coins over which the children eagerly scuffled. "Bide your time."

"God bless you, my lord," said one of the older men. "God bless you and your many sons!"

Why did everyone speak of sons? thought Kate disjointedly.

A cobbled road led up through orchards of fruit trees and past a pond in which swans, white and black, swam languidly. They passed a stone wall, overgrown with vines, around what looked like a smaller, private garden, and Kate caught a glimpse of another young man as he stepped through the open gate toward them and then ducked back inside as if to prevent his being seen. He was a tall fellow with shaggy, sandy hair. She wondered why he'd disappeared like that and what he had to hide.

After a short while, Henry stopped his horse, dismounted, and then helped Kate down from the pony. He has a broad, handsome face, she thought, his skin flushed and healthy from the sun. For a moment, he was close enough for her to breathe his scent: sage and peppermint, a clean, forest smell. Her knees felt weak but it wasn't because of the ride. She was tempted to lean even closer to him, but then she regained her senses and pulled away, just as two young men ran over to take the horses.

"Give them a good rubdown," her companion said. "They've had a fine workout today." As the grooms led the horses toward the stables, Henry contemplated Kate.

"You are keeping your arrival secret?" he asked. "You must have paid your servants well to accompany you to Greenwich in secret."

"I don't know what you mean," Kate hedged, stumbling on the stones.

"You did not make the journey by yourself?" he asked, his voice concerned. "There are dangers about, especially for

Arthur's widow. I will send word regarding your whereabouts, for when you are discovered missing, there will be great consternation."

"Arthur's—" she began, then stopped. A sadness not her own squeezed her heart, preventing her from continuing.

"Katherine, you are some changed," he continued, after a minute. "I heard you had not been well, but ... my brother's widow would not normally look so—"

"But I'm not! I—" Kate interrupted, and then stopped. She couldn't let him think that she was a relative—and a widow, at that! But what could she tell him—that she didn't have a clue where she was or what she was doing here? And then something in her responded to his words, allowed her to say, "It is all right, Henry. What matters is that I am here now, and quite well."

"But you are bleeding!" he exclaimed, examining her scratched hand.

One of the nearby gardeners, wearing a plain tunic and leggings, turned from his hoe and stared. Kate fell silent under his scrutiny. Her companion called, "Master Walsh, how are the apples?" and the gardener indicated, with a flourish of his arm, a basket of wizened fruit that stood near their feet. "Take what you want, Prince Henry," he said. "With my good blessing." *Prince Henry,* thought Kate.

"Bear them to the kitchens," said Henry dismissively, "that they may be made into tarts for our supper." Anxious to overcome her thoughts, Kate leaned over and took an apple, but before she could bite into it, Henry looked at her, aghast.

"You won't be eating raw fruit, Katherine!" he exclaimed. "Raw fruit causes an abundance of cold, wet humors ... please, take care."

Kate quickly dropped the apple back into the basket. Numbly, she followed Henry up the path to the palace, every now and then meeting his worried glance as he turned back to study her. As they passed into an inner courtyard, she had a momentary rush of claustrophobia, and, for reassurance, turned over her left palm, studying the white scar. Henry took up her hand and brought it to his lips, then unfolded it and looked at the palm.

"*H* for *Henry*," he said, playfully.

With a sharp intake of breath, she looked at the scar. What she'd always thought of as a K now startled her in its resemblance to an H. Or maybe it had always looked like an H. Her head began to spin.

"We will hasten to your nurse," said Henry, beckoning her under a stone arch. "I trust that she will know how to mend you." Kate had the feeling that he was referring to more than the scratch from the pup, but she was too distracted by her thoughts to think about it very deeply. She looked up, trying to catch her breath. Picturesque brick work, mullioned windows, and stately gables loomed over her, along with gargoyles grinning down as if to share some secret joke.

At the same time as it all seemed grand and terrifying, she intuitively led the way through the maze of passages and doorways to the upper level, where she found the final doorway into rooms she knew well. She touched her hand to her aching eyes.

I must be careful what I say, thought Kate feverishly, following Henry into a room hung with rich tapestries. An older woman was standing beside one of the walls, rubbing with a husk of bread a section of a large, intricately designed wall hanging. When she turned and saw Henry, she immediately threw down the bread.

"Well, well, imagine me, an old woman, cleaning our own tapestries." She leaned toward the wall and brushed away a few of the leftover crumbs. "Do you not think that we deserve more help in these rooms? Whether Katherine is here or not?" Then she saw Kate behind Henry. Her snapping brown eyes took in Kate's expression with what might have been an answering look of fear. Then she lowered her eyelids and clicked her tongue, bustling Kate into the next room, where she bathed her face and hands in a bowl of rose-scented water and dabbed at the scratches with a handkerchief. The woman's skin was weathered dark and wrinkled and she looked about sixty, although Kate wondered if she might be younger on account of the jet black hair that was fastened under an embroidered velvet head piece. Kate's gaze fastened on dark hairs that erupted from the older woman's chin, but rather than seeing these with surprise, her reaction was instead one of familiarity.

This is Doña Elvira, thought Kate foggily. *My nurse. She is married to Don Pedro Manrique, but she stays here with me when she's needed, and lives with him in their other rooms downstairs when I'm away. I wonder where the other maids are! They should be here, helping, unless they've been sent away with the sweating sickness* ... She swallowed and put her hand back up to her throbbing eyes.

"Oh, it's not a good thing to see you back so soon," Doña Elvira muttered. "There'll be trouble because of it, mark my words." Although Doña Elvira's speech when she spoke to her privately like this sounded strange and foreign, Kate understood every word. It was as if the nurse were speaking in another language, but a language somehow very familiar.

After Doña Elvira had cleaned her up, she covered Kate's head with a blue silk hood and then tied a red ribbon around her wrist: "To ward off bad luck," she muttered. Then she gave her something to drink—something tart and sweet at the same time—and sternly told her to sit down on the bed. Kate felt too heavy to resist as Doña Elvira removed her shoes, looking at them with a horrified glance.

"What have you got on your feet?" she croaked. Then her gaze moved upward to the jeans under Kate's dress.

"And what are you wearing on your legs! The cloth is thick, like bark!"

That could be used in an advertisement, Kate thought, hysterical laughter rising in her chest. *Denim bark, the newest fad. Do not wash, but allow to weather appropriately. Grows along with the wearer.*

"Not even fit for the grooms," muttered Doña Elvira, tugging at the jeans. Kate dizzily assisted their removal and watched the old woman pitch them, along with the runners, into a corner of the room.

"Good thing I've aired your slippers," muttered Doña Elvira. She left the room for a few minutes and Kate felt her eyes drooping shut. Suddenly Doña Elvira returned with a white cotton shift.

"Put this on and take some rest. We'll see what we can make of you this afternoon," she commanded. Then she went back to Henry. Kate held the garment but didn't move, listening to their conversation in the other room.

"Henry, what has happened? Why is our princess back from Fulham Palace?" Kate heard the old woman's question very clearly but couldn't make out the answer. Something in the drink was making her very drowsy, and her only desire was to sleep as she had been commanded to do. She made a feeble attempt to undress, but her arms were too heavy; instead, she tumbled over onto cool linen sheets and shut her eyes.

13
The meal

When Kate awoke, her body felt stiff and sore, as if she had been sleeping a long time. She was in the same strange bed and she could see by the window that it was dusk. The room was dimly lit by a single lantern in the corner and she could smell the thick aroma of burning oil. Kate's mind was immediately a hive for buzzing thoughts. Here she was in this peculiar place with people who thought she was someone else. Could she ever get home?

She looked at the nightgown in her hands and wondered if she should put it on, but she couldn't seem to make her body take orders. Pain ebbed and flowed in her left temple. When she moved, the headache worsened. Whatever she'd been given to drink, she'd best not drink any more of it.

"I'm going down to dinner," she heard a woman say in a voice that sounded like dry reeds rubbing together. "Will she be all right if we leave her alone?"

"Yes, most certainly," came Doña Elvira's distinctive cadences. "If she saw a cunning woman and the cat's got her tongue, there are remedies for that."

"Do you think herself's a sorcerer?" a third woman cried. There was fear in her voice.

"No, of course not! Stop the talk this instant." That was Doña Elvira again, speaking very firmly.

"I didn't mean ... but will she soon be well?" It was Reedy Voice again.

"Soon, by St. Sebastian. She's a strong girl. It won't take long. We'll use the leeches if need be. It is good to have her home in these difficult times," replied Doña Elvira.

Kate shivered under the damp covers and waited until she heard the women retreat down the corridor. Then curiosity and reason got the better of fear. She needed to get up and figure things out. These people were obviously suspicious of her and, wherever she was, if people thought she was a witch, that could be dangerous. Fenwick had made them study this at school, how witches had been burned at the stake. Kate rolled over and thrust her legs off the bed, her feet just touching the floor. Then, standing up shakily, her head pounding, she peered out into the sitting room. It was empty. The bread had been removed and the tile floor swept clean. A small fire glowed in some sort of fire pan, chunks of charcoal sending off an inviting warmth.

Kate determinedly took a deep breath, shook off the dizziness, and sneaked through the sitting room and down the stone passageway toward a thick stream of voices. Soon she was peering through a doorway into a great room whose roof timbers were painted yellow ochre. The smell hit her hard, and it wasn't a pleasant one. A bitter combination of human sweat and acrid odors from the rushes on the floor brought tears to her eyes. Long rows of people—about three hundred in all, Kate estimated—sat at trestle tables, and servants in aprons and caps came and went, carrying silver and gold serving dishes. There was a constant tide of laughter and clattering utensils, with boisterous conversations that rose and fell.

Kate turned her head away from the stench, her stomach turning unpleasantly. A thick fishy odor that wafted over from a nearby table made her wonder if the meat was entirely fresh. She wrinkled her nose, staring back at the throng as a gaudily dressed clown tumbled head over heels up and down the aisles. Music wove in and out of the sea of voices. At the far end of the room, a man was playing a tubby-looking guitar and singing. Kate gradually noticed other milder smells that were rather pleasant. Violets, she thought, looking down at the rushes. Then she glanced back at the tables, following the pungent scent of sage. She watched as a woman in a low-necked long gown cut her food with a knife, poked bits into her mouth with her fingers, and then threw the bones at her feet. Did nobody eat with forks? Kate looked around, her neck and back beginning to ache from the angle at which she stood in the doorway, trying to remain unnoticed. Decisively, she crept into the room and slipped into an empty chair. Either she could pass freely here, or she'd be undone—might as well find out.

At her right, a heated conversation seemed to be brewing between two portly gentlemen dressed in plain brown cloth.

"Kings of England have never had ... never had any superior except God!" said the bald-headed one, his words slurring a bit because, Kate thought, of the ale he was thirstily gulping down. "What makes you think His Majesty ... is any different?"

"I'm not questioning that his ... that his superior is God," said the second, his words equally slurred. He spat onto the floor and then used his foot to tread the glob into the rushes. He lowered his voice and Kate could hardly hear the next part. "What I'm saying is that His Highness seized the crown from King Richard, who also served God. Both served God, yet one triumphed and the other perished. How is that possible?"

"Mind your tongues and pass a little more of the venison," brayed a middle-aged lady from across the table, burping loudly. "Remember, you're in the King's hall," she chided, then smiled at Kate. "Have you eaten, luv? Try the venison; it is particularly good."

"Of course, we meant no harm," said the second man nervously, but the first had already poured himself another glass of ale.

"Now this is what my two lips are hankering for," the woman said, pulling meat from the serving tray.

"Are you sure it's venison they'll be after, truly?" cried the first man with a loud guffaw.

"What about a kiss?" offered the second man, winking.

"Thank you kindly," said the woman, her mouth full. "But I have enough kisses promised from ..." Kate couldn't hear the name she gave, but the two men seemed chastened and poured themselves more ale. "And I even have some of the lamb left for the beggars," the woman said. She beckoned over one of the serving girls, who scraped the meat from the plate into a basin.

Kate remembered the children crowded around the palace gates and hoped they would all be taken care of, although eating someone's leftovers wasn't her idea of healthy charity. The contrast between excess and poverty bothered her. And the smell, wafting over to her from the dining population, was less than encouraging—the odor of hot, unwashed bodies, old sweat on fabric, and greasy hair. Kate's stomach lurched. She stood up, afraid she was going to be sick, as a woman with long, thin arms held a gold-filigreed ball up to her nose and breathed deeply. Uncannily, Kate knew what it would smell like—a thick musk, temporarily taking away the unpleasantly human scents nearby.

She quickly went back to the corridor and leaned against its cool stone wall. After a few moments, feeling better, she peered once again into the room. Her attention was drawn to the jester's somersaults. In a moment, he began to do back flips, rushes sticking to his colorful cap. A couple of men hooted approval, and then another cleared his throat and spat onto the floor at the jester's feet.

"Pass the ale!" cried he. "Before it's emptied!"

Kate thought the fellow had likely had enough of anything alcoholic, but saw a serving maid bustle over with what appeared to be a full tankard. Kate stood, mesmerized, staring first at the man as he tipped the container and guzzled noisily its contents, next at the jester, now making his way back to the front of the room, and then at the throng that obviously had all been taught the same unusual table manners. People left and right were chewing loudly, spitting, and scratching various body parts. *My father the King,* she thought. *Prince Henry. Princess Katherine.* Parallels to the characters in Willow's play rushed at her. *Henry and Katherine. Katherine the Queen,* who died from cancer of the heart. *King Henry the eighth to six wives he was wedded: one died, one survived, two divorced, two beheaded.*

She forced herself to observe the people in the room, taking pains to learn their habits. Until she could get away, she'd better know how to behave, or the superstitions about witches would be her downfall. She remembered reading somewhere that witch-hunts used to be common. But she couldn't remember the time period when witches were hunted down and killed. Just how. And it was gruesome. People tied a bag of stones around the neck of an accused witch and threw her into a pond. If she floated, she was a witch and then had to be burned. If she sank, she was not a witch but had probably by that time drowned. *What century am I in*? she thought, unsuccessfully trying to remember what Willow had told her about Tudor times.

If she could pass successfully for Katherine just for a while, it would give her the chance to find a way to escape. And it was just a matter of studying people, she mused. Doing what others did. Trying to fit in. You ate with a knife and your fingers, using the left hand to take food from communal dishes and extending the thumb and first two fingers of the right hand for bringing the food to your mouth. The knife was also used for serving and cutting meat, and helping yourself to salt bowls.

Kate suddenly remembered that she hadn't tried very hard to fit in when she'd moved to London. *Big Apple*; the name still stung. Had she been the snob that her sister accused her of being? But that familiar London world was not part of this world at all. With sudden relief she realized that all the old heartaches—her mother's abandonment, her father's death—were part of another life. Almost as if they had never happened. And, in truth, if she were in some past time, they really had not happened. Not yet. The thought brought a kind of freedom and, with it, great peace.

As she watched even more closely the events in the dining hall, she began to identify the courses that servants carried to the tables. First had been a number of different types of meat; there were hefty legs of lamb, long trays of meat pies, and the venison she'd seen the woman eating, as well as baskets of round, dark loaves of bread. After the first serving dishes were taken away, she saw plates of fish and other meat, as well as more bread, and then tarts and white pudding in small pottery bowls. And when people finished their meal, it wasn't uncommon for diners to use a toothpick while sitting at the table—even while leaning over serving bowls from which others were still eating—talking and laughing with friends.

One thing she noticed was that people didn't consume the shells when they ate the meat pies. It looked as if the crusts were used as bowls. After people had eaten out the filling, they threw the rest on the ground for dogs to eat, and there were a great number of dogs to oblige.

A woman in a fine low-cut silver dress was paying a great deal of attention to the large dog leaning at her legs. A greyhound, Kate identified by its slender body. Every now and then the woman would pass it a tidbit of meat, which it ate very delicately. The woman stroked its silky neck and then suddenly turned aside, holding a pomander to her nose. Apparently, Kate guessed, as others from the table fanned the air and drew away from the animal, the dog had passed gas.

"Got yourself a live one there," someone at the table called out.

"My aunt had a greyhound that could clear a whole room," called someone else.

Kate thought of her history teacher and smiled.

"So there you are," came a voice from behind her in the corridor, startling her out of her reverie. "Are you feeling better?"

She turned and felt her cheeks tingle pleasantly at Henry's tone. Then she nodded, glancing shyly into his electric blue eyes.

"There's ... there's a great deal of meat served here," she stammered. Why could she never think of the right thing to say to a boy?

"But of course. We must show visitors the King's power," he said, looking at her curiously. She pressed her lips together. Of course, this was something Katherine would know.

Thoughts that were Katherine's impressed themselves on her consciousness. *When one considers the work that goes into roasting meat, and sees the results on fine tables, one cannot help but be impressed.*

Kate looked up again at the high ceiling of the hall, feeling small and insignificant, as she was meant to do. *This fine hall was built to show the King's power and might, and cause people of the court to feel mean in comparison.*

"Why are those roses all over the ceiling?" she blurted.

"Did not Arthur explain any of this?" Henry asked slowly, guiding her back into the hall, intent on the subject of her question.

"Your Highness, it is wonderful to see you this evening," said the woman with the greyhound, and others at the tabled murmured agreement, bowing their heads and otherwise showing deference by clasping their hands over their hearts.

The mention of Arthur's name had sent a chill down Kate's spine and her legs felt weak. Again she saw the black carriage drawn by dark horses and felt an awful shuddery feeling inside her chest. Henry, still intent on her, was expecting an answer, so Kate shook her head. "The Tudor rose represents two great families coming together," he went on. "Lancaster, my father, and York. York for ... for my mother." The way he said *my mother* made Kate glance at his face. It was suddenly drawn with a pain Kate recognized from her own heart's past. His mother's dead, she said to herself.

"I have arranged for food to be brought to your chamber, thinking you might not want to be in company," Henry said, in quite a different tone. "I understand that you are here in secret from the King, as it was at his bidding that you went away. And your secret can be kept a little while longer, as His Majesty is busy with guests from France. Don't worry. No one else will care that you have returned a bit early." He drew her back into the corridor where he stopped and looked at her with fondness. "Did you miss me that much, then?"

She blushed harder.

"Confound it, I would like to know you better!" he exclaimed. "You are quite extraordinary."

If I'm dreaming, I should just wake up, she thought. *Wake up before it's too late!* She squeezed her eyes tightly shut. When she opened them after a few tense seconds, she was still standing in the passageway, light from the torches casting dancing shadows along the walls. She squeezed her eyes shut again.

"Do you have something in your eye?" Henry asked, offering her a white handkerchief.

She shook her head and he took a step closer. There it was again—a fresh smell of sage and mint that made her knees feel like jelly. He placed his hand under her chin and lifted her face up to his. Their lips touched. She felt the world around her sway. Then she drew back.

"Maybe we should return to ..." she began weakly, her head throbbing. This wasn't at all like kissing Hal. It was a hundred times better.

"Yes, yes, and get you your dinner. You must be starving." Henry led the way back down the narrow corridor, and soon Kate was dining on thick slices of bread, cabbage, baked apples, and pieces of tender, salty meat. Since there were no forks, she used her fingers as she had seen the people do back in the hall. Her hunger from hours earlier was finally eased, along with her headache, and she thought that never had she had a meal as good as this.

"What meat is this?" she asked, her mouth half-full.

"Peacock," answered Henry jauntily. "Can't you tell?"

14
The memories

"Peacock!" choked Kate, but Henry went on, oblivious to her reaction. "I would have brought you the tail but that swine of a tutor carried off the feathers to make pens." He suddenly stopped and looked at her more seriously. "Your horse is well attended in the stables. The grooms have given her a fresh stall."

"My horse?" exclaimed Kate.

Henry sent her a measured glance and she quickly added, "Thank you," remembering the dappled gray mare *that I have ridden these last six years*. Again, another memory had magically superimposed itself on her own. She had to be very careful. Who knew what these people would do if they thought she really was a witch?

"You've been kind," she said simply, with as much dignity as she could muster.

His appraising glance made her blush again and look down at her plate.

"Women generally do not have such courage," he said. "But I must know about your hair. Why has it been cut?"

Kate reached up and touched her hair. It was shorter than Katherine was used to, but the same as always to Kate. Was it possible to live so divided?

"I ... I wanted to pass about more freely," she mumbled, touching the offending strands of auburn.

"You are not feeding her, Henry?" Doña Elvira bustled in with a tray. "I brought a white custard, which would have been softer on the stomach."

"I'll have it, too," Kate said, wanting to oblige. She thought about this other Katherine whose world had blended so crazily with her own. While Kate had entered Tudor times, where had Katherine gone? Had she left the tunnel at Kate's point of entry and then stayed in Kate's time, to live with Willow? Kate shoveled in a spoonful of pudding, and then another, wondering suddenly how Katherine would be managing with the soup.

Doña Elvira raised her eyebrows. "Don't make a hog of yourself," she said tartly, "or you will spoil your figure. What you need is a simple diet, rest, quiet, and some exercise. I'll take that"—she added, grabbing Kate's half-full pudding dish—"for the voider. The Almoner is waiting to feed the beggars and we all must do our duty. Now: rest, quiet, and exercise," she repeated, giving Henry a sharp look. Henry took the hint and stood.

"We will play tennis in the morning," he said, "and see if you are still a match for me. And I must show you something I have acquired," he whispered softly when Doña Elvira stepped deferentially into the other room. Kate raised her eyebrows as he added, "An astrolabe!"

"An astrolabe. What's that?" she asked. He looked oddly shaken at her words. "Oh, an astrolabe," she repeated. "I misheard you, at first. I thought you said ..." she struggled to think of a replacement. "Something else."

"Being that it has such amazing accuracy in calculating a ship's position," he looked at Kate even more searchingly, "you do remember us speaking of it, don't you?"

"Of course," Kate said. He nodded and then spoke more brusquely.

"I was thinking of your birthday ... when is the actual date, Katherine?"

"December 16," Kate said automatically. This seemed to surprise him, but he looked relieved and then smiled.

"Ah, yes, the correct date," he murmured. "All is well, then, with your memory."

Kate swallowed hard. He was certainly testing her. But all was clearly not well with her memory! Her fifteenth birthday was on Monday, October 16. Not December 16. Why had she said *December*? It was the same as when she'd known the way to these rooms, and when she'd recognized the gray pony, and when she'd felt that, indeed, her hair *had* been cut. She was confusingly two different people, Katherine and Kate, inexplicably entwined.

Henry turned to Doña Elvira, who had bustled back into the room. "Get her a different dress," he commanded. "With her hair short, and Grandmother's ladies busy with the King's visitors from France, and the King himself similarly engaged, she will pass about without drawing their attention."

Doña Elvira nodded, her sharp eyes flickering back and forth between Henry and Kate.

Henry continued in a gentler tone. "By the time her presence is noticed, the reasons for her going may be out of date."

"Lady Margaret, no doubt, will be too busy to consider more servants for us now the princess has returned?" said Doña Elvira.

"Indeed, my grandmother is at the moment fully occupied," Henry replied regretfully but with authority.

He's good at making hard decisions, Kate thought. Reminds me of Willow. And suddenly Willow seemed very far away. Then she realized that Katherine would have to go to the Camden school on Monday in her place! They might not burn her at the stake, but they surely could make her roast a little. She felt dangerous laughter bubbling up in her throat.

"See you in the morning?" said Henry.

"Tennis," Kate answered, swallowing hard and catching

Doña Elvira's sharp look. "Uh ... thank you for the ride back today, and for your ... uh ... consideration."

"I did nothing that any honorable man would not have done," said Henry gently. "Sleep well." His gaze made Kate want to throw her arms around him, but she caught a glimpse of an item on a leather thong around his neck and looked at it curiously. It was the tooth of some predatory animal. A shark, or perhaps a lion.

Henry looked at Kate for another moment and she felt his magnetic power. When she made no motion to step forward, however, he reluctantly turned and left the room. A sick feeling churned in her stomach as she gave herself completely to the thoughts she'd been harboring all day. Prince Henry. Princess Katherine.

"Princess? Princess!" Kate was only vaguely aware of Doña Elvira's scolding words as her mind spun back and forth the threads she had gathered. She, Kate, had actually gone back to Tudor times, as Katherine of Aragon. It was completely and ridiculously clear—she was somehow, right now, in another century. But how could this handsome guy become the Henry VIII her sister had been talking about? The horrible tyrant and murderer who'd had six wives?

"What's the matter with you!" Doña Elvira continued. "Too good for him all of a sudden? You had better take care, young lady; you had just better take care. And tonight you will wear this," she continued, stuffing a piece of fur down Kate's back.

"What—?" cried Kate.

Doña Elvira shook her head. "For the bedbugs to eat, of course. You are worrying me. I might have to bleed you in the morning if you are not returned to health. Oh, Katherine, try to recover yourself." Doña Elvira's tone became more authoritative. "Our position here in court depends on you. We both are quite aware that it does. If anything should happen to you, our Spanish envoy would be quite undone."

"Bleed me?" stammered Kate. "Like with leeches?" The old woman nodded. "Oh, I'm sure I'll be fine," Kate insisted. "You're right, I really just need rest." She went obediently into the other room where she stood, twisting her hands. Like Katherine of Aragon had once been, Kate was new in this court but, unlike Katherine, Kate might not be able to fit in so easily. She climbed up on one side of the big four-poster bed, drawing the covers up to conceal her gown, for she would need to be fully dressed to engineer her escape once everyone went to bed. If only she could remember the route back to the tunnel—for that might be her only passage home! In a few minutes, she was startled to see Doña Elvira climbing up on the other side of the bed.

"Sleep well, then," croaked the old woman, echoing Henry.

"You ... you're going to sleep here? In this bed?" Kate asked.

"For as long as you need me, just like old times," said Doña Elvira kindly. "Good night. And remember to sleep with your mouth open, to keep the breath sweet."

"Good ... good night," Kate stammered. She lay back, observing what quite possibly was a nightly ritual, as Doña Elvira plucked out as many of her own chin hairs as she could grasp between the nails of her thumb and index finger. The routine began with some intensity that faded as the old woman relaxed.

As soon as Doña Elvira was snoring beside her, Kate rolled from under the quilts and tiptoed barefoot around the room, itchier than she had ever been in her life and wondering if the fur hadn't actually attracted fleas and bedbugs to her skin. Kate squeezed on Katherine's footwear with a small sigh. The shoes Doña Elvira had given her to wear were not comfortable, and she longed for her running shoes, but they, along with her jeans, were nowhere to be seen.

When her eyes had adjusted to the dim light, Kate crept stealthily down the corridor of the palace, sniffing at the cool, damp smell that had intensified with the darkness. This place could use a better ventilation system, she thought. Lanterns set in the walls cast flickering shadows across her path and she inhaled the hot, dusty stench of burning oil. She didn't encounter anyone except one of the serving maids, scuttling quickly along with something under one arm. It looked like an embroidered cloth of some kind, and, in what Kate saw was a fit of terror, the girl dropped it on the ground, then hastily retrieved it as a loaf of bread fell out.

"Never mind," said Kate, seeing the fear on the girl's face. "Never mind, it's all right."

In response, the girl shoved the bread at her, crying, "Don't tell. Oh, please ... don't tell!" before she scurried off, hugging the cloth close to her chest.

"Hey!" called Kate. "Come back! Take this with you!" But the girl had disappeared. Kate looked at the bread. Stale and crusty, it was no doubt meant for someone who was hungry enough not to mind its texture or its taste.

At last, Kate took a deep breath of fresh air, feeling the dank oiliness of the palace rooms leave her lungs. Then she headed down the moonlit path, hoping that Katherine's knowledge would help her to find and saddle the gray pony. She would somehow have to make her way back to the tunnel—if only she could! It wasn't far, if she could just remember the right course.

The full moon hung in the sky like a great orange lantern; it, and Katherine's recollections of the grounds helped her to see her way in the direction of the stables. As she neared the gardens, she quickened her pace, afraid someone would discover her here, out in the open and away from the more populated areas of the palace.

When she bumped into the tall young man coming around the side of a garden wall, it was with such force that she stumbled and almost fell. Catching herself, she quickly stepped back with a startled exclamation. He gave an echoing exclamation as he struggled with his balance. She saw in his hands a loaf of bread like her own, and an incredulous giggle burst from her lips.

"I beg your pardon!" he said, brushing sandy hair from his eyes.

"I saw you this morning!" blurted Kate. He was the same fellow she'd seen emerging from the gate when she and Henry had ridden past, the one who'd taken care to hide himself.

"Are you ... you have brought ..." he stammered, staring at the bread she carried. Then he took her arm and drew her inside the gate.

"Quickly, then, let's inside before someone spies us here," he said, leading the way toward a small thatched shed.

Deftly, the young man lit a match and held it to a candle that was on the window ledge. In the flickering light, Kate took in the garden tools, bowls of seeds, and then, on the floor, she saw the wolf cub, curled up on an old piece of sacking. It opened one eye and surveyed them balefully, its strange, pale face tilted up like a baby bird's.

"Oh, Princess Katherine! I'm ... I'm very sorry, I did not recognize you a moment ago," stammered the young man, giving her a little bow. "Please forgive me for being so ... so forward."

"It is quite all right, William," she said, accepting the

knowledge that flowed from Katherine's memories. She tried to remember his last name but was unsuccessful. He bent down, perhaps to cover his embarrassment, and dipped some of his bread in water and then offered it to the cub, who lapped at it hungrily.

"So, you have discovered my secret," said William, darting a quick look at her face. "And ... you are ... you are not unhappy with the arrangement?"

"What?" she asked.

"You are ... you ... you support the care of this young creature?" he stammered.

Kate nodded. "Absolutely. There is no reason for it to suffer."

His face seemed to relax and he contemplated her more obviously.

"Was there a sound that set you to find him here?" he asked.

"No—" Kate started, and then realized it was going to be difficult to explain the fact of being out, carrying bread. "Well, I saw you earlier when we rode by," she said. "I just guessed."

"Quite a deduction," he said. "I remember you once speaking to Prince Henry about the hunt. But then you were more concerned for foxes."

"Yes!" said Kate, trying to match his memories with ones she was hurriedly inventing. "And the Prince talked of other royal hunts in other courts."

William looked confused. "Other hunts?"

"In Asia, don't they hunt lions?" said Kate.

"In Asia?" he repeated.

Kate knew she was in over her head. Maybe the English had not yet discovered Asia. Why hadn't she paid more attention at school?

"I thought the wolves were all gone," she blurted.

"As did I," he replied. "But you can't be a hundred percent certain about anything, as we have discovered." *Not a hundred percent certain. About anything, really,* Martin had said in another place at another time.

William's tone was formal, and Kate wondered what the history was between them. Other than the obvious five hundred years, she thought wryly. They had not been close friends, she was sure, but Katherine seemed to trust William. As a friend of Henry's, he was ... reliable. The word popped into her head and seemed to fit him perfectly.

"When I saw the pelts all stacked up at MacQueen's, I felt sick to my stomach," she said honestly, recalling the horrible smell of the rubbish heap. She was queasy even now, remembering. She looked back at the little creature whose neck muscles seemed too weak to hold up its head. *Poor little thing.*

"I have been sickened by the extermination of wolves for as long as I can remember," confided William. "Years ago, my father fenced some of our land off for sheep, and although we had some concern, wolves were never a problem as long as we watched over the sheep by day and brought them into their enclosures at night." He scratched his arm and then continued, more slowly. "That's the secret to keeping sheep, unless you are the kind of farmer who cries wolf to cover up your lazy habits."

"Like the boy who cried wolf," said Kate, thinking of the children's story.

"What?" said William.

"Where is your father's land?" asked Kate to divert him, sitting down beside the cub and stroking its tawny back.

"Some distance away, beside the Thames," he replied, "where the land is drier and more suitable for ungulates." He scratched again, the other arm this time.

"Ungulates?" asked Kate.

"Sheep," he said and smiled. "I sometimes forget that everyone does not share my store of farming knowledge. My apologies."

"And why aren't you there now, looking after sheep, instead of here at the castle?" she asked, thinking how easy it was to talk to this fellow. The sandy-haired lad dropped his head.

"I thought you knew," he said, softly. "Father was arrested to the Tower three years ago, and because mother is a cousin of Elizabeth of York, I was offered a position here at the royal palace as one of Prince Henry's companions. As his cup-bearer, actually, but I'm invited to study alongside, which is not an easy assignment." He picked a flea from inside his sleeve, looked at it, and then squashed it unceremoniously between thumb and forefinger.

"And why was your father arrested?" asked Kate, hearing a gentle tone in her voice that surprised her.

"He was suspected of treason," William replied. "But he's innocent! He was accused of working to locate the Plantagenet nephews of Richard III—but that is preposterous. Father is a farmer, and loyal to Henry VII. Whoever's been spreading rumors about him is crooked. Someday I'll prove that to them all and he'll be released. I hope," he added fervently.

"I'm sorry," said Kate. "I hope so, too." She had vague recollections of a story about two children in the Tower of London but couldn't remember any details. Why hadn't she gone on that tour! Then she'd be much more prepared for what she was experiencing now!

William looked at her for a moment and then turned his attention back to the cub.

"God be willing, he'll be released," he repeated, but Kate knew he wasn't referring to the animal.

They watched the wolf for a few minutes until it had eaten its fill. Kate dipped the remaining bread in water, softening it and then setting it beside the bowl for the cub to eat later.

Then she stood up, brushing the straw from her skirts.

"I should be going," she said, wondering how she could get to the stable from here.

"I'll accompany you back," said William, courteously holding open the door and curtailing any further plans for tonight.

"I hope it will be safe," she said, looking over at the helpless creature. William nodded, snuffed out the candle, and then followed her out of the hut.

"As long as it's eating and drinking, it'll come round," he said. "That one's got a strong heart, I can tell that much. And the will to live."

The moon shone brightly on the path, making the stones underfoot a ghostly white. Kate wondered fearfully if anyone inside the castle could hear their footsteps and tried to walk quietly, but William's passage was so noisy she was sure he was waking everyone. She looked up at the walls looming above them, and the feeling of being small and insignificant washed over her again.

"It's quite a place, is it not?" said William. "I heard it cost the Tudors nine hundred pounds to employ the master mason and his men when the castle was rebuilt."

"Indeed," said Kate, the formal response occurring almost naturally.

"I'd rather be out under the stars, if the truth be known," said William, "than sleeping inside this place. For if a fire came upon us, in minutes we'd be burnt to cinders. Well ..." and here he stopped at the door to the great hall, "good night."

"Good night," she said in return, stifling a sudden urge to laugh at his quick change of heart, one minute predicting doom, the next cheerfully bidding her adieu. William headed away to the rooms he shared with others of his standing, while Kate waited, pondering her next step. Inside the hall, Kate could see servants sleeping on the floor, and, by the light of a few lanterns, she could also see mice, or maybe rats, scampering among the rushes. Strengthening her resolve, she determined to get herself out of here. Chest tight in a sudden burst of urgency, she turned to go back outside when a familiar voice caught her by surprise.

"Well, look what the cat dragged in." Doña Elvira's tone was fierce and, with a sinking heart, Kate knew she'd have to try her escape plan another night. Her feet ached in the borrowed shoes; she'd better get her own shoes back as soon as possible.

"I couldn't sleep," she said weakly. "And felt a bit of night air would do me good."

"The night air will kill you soon as heal you," snapped the old woman. "Come with me. We're needed on the Queen's side. One of Lady Margaret's own is due."

"Prince Henry's Grandma is giving birth?" said Kate stupidly.

"Not Lady Margaret, of course! One of her maids!"

"Having a baby? One of her maids is having a baby? Here?"

"Well, where would you expect?" snapped Doña Elvira. "In the sky? Now hurry up."

"Well, I could just go back to bed—" started Kate eagerly.

"You'll stay with me," was the tight-lipped response. "Fool girl wandering about at night. Tomorrow I'll see about the leeches."

Tired and disappointed, Kate limped after Doña Elvira through dimly lit corridors until they reached Lady Margaret's apartments. These were more richly furnished than their own rooms, with thick red and gold hangings on the walls. She guessed the floors were marble and there were velvet carpets strewn about. Like her own chambers, the walls were plastered brick, but in some of the bigger rooms she could see linen-like paneling and, in one very big room, a brilliant tapestry that must be fifty feet long. It depicted a scene from the Bible, Kate thought, recognizing the style from a children's picture book she'd had in New York. Up a stone staircase were the more private bedchambers and, in one of these, a young woman lay moaning on a pallet of straw. Doña Elvira checked her under the gaze of four other wide-eyed maids and then sighed.

"Well, there won't be a baby born this night. Just too many suckets eaten at dinner." She drew open her bag and produced a leather packet. "Mix this powder in water and give it to her every hour until the pains diminish. Come and get me if there are any new symptoms."

"What was the remedy?" asked Kate, feeling a cramp settling in her own stomach from the night's excitement.

"Powdered sapphires," said Doña Elvira.

15
The mathematics of loss

"Sapphires are useful in case there's a touch of the sweating sickness," Doña Elvira continued. "I doubt very much this is the case. There's certainly no labor and, since it's early, I won't give her any juniper. With God's grace, we'll have a few more weeks of resting-in before that baby is born."

"Oh," said Kate, shocked at the idea of eating sapphires. She'd better not complain of any illness or who knows what she'd be given as a remedy.

Soon she found herself back under the covers with her strange bedfellow, observing again the ritual picking of the beard. This time, Kate was exhausted, but instead of dropping right off to sleep, her mind swirled with bits and pieces of the day. What if the tunnel worked as a kind of elevator, an elevator that started and stopped at particular points in its respective universes? If this were true, she could go back to her own place and time at the original point of exit. Except that the other Katherine was there. Taking her place. The idea was mathematically sound. The princess and she had merely changed sides on their universal axes.

Dizzily, she wondered what the princess intended to do. Once Kate crossed back into her own time, could she and Katherine both stay there? As identical twins or something? Romantically, the idea of being an identical twin separated at birth took hold. Then her mind jumped haphazardly to what she would have to do to manage her escape.

Her eye fell on a brass candelabra that was standing on a shelf by the bed, its three candles flickering on burnt stubs. What if she used it as a weapon and smashed Doña Elvira on the head? As soon as the idea occurred, Kate knew she could never go through with it. Doña Elvira had been with Katherine ever since she was a child, and Kate sensed that Katherine loved Doña Elvira better than she loved anyone. Memories rushed in before Kate could stop them, and her heart beat faster as she tried to keep her perspective, and Katherine's, separate and distinct.

On the boat, Katherine had been miserably seasick. Doña Elvira had sat beside the bed, reading from the Bible and offering drinks of water. Sometimes she'd placed a cool cloth on Katherine's forehead; sometimes she'd rubbed her wrists and arms to keep them from cramping.

In this new place, it had been Doña Elvira who'd encouraged her, promised that she'd get more and more comfortable as time went on. And she'd been right. Katherine was comfortable here. She didn't want to live anywhere else and hoped she could fulfill whatever role God intended for her. And she loved Prince Henry.

The memory of the door rose again in Kate's thoughts, an even clearer picture than she'd had in the tunnel. It was a big wooden door, ornately carved and tightly shut. She was standing outside, awaiting a message. The message was something to do with her future here. She wanted the door to open but, at the same time, she wanted it to stay shut. If there was to be bad news, perhaps it was better not to know. The King might choose her as Henry's bride or he might cast her as Arthur's widow for the rest of her life. Whatever her fate was, it was in the King's hands.

The image of the door was smoothly replaced in Kate's mind with other things. The apple blossoms in the orchard in spring, when all you had to do was walk beneath the trees to have a petal crown delivered by the wind. A long white dress that hung somewhere just out of reach. The taste of lemons, freshly squeezed on the creamy fish that was served on long pewter plates, carried to the table by someone in red livery.

Lemons. The thought of them snapped Kate back into the old fear, darkness welling up in her throat until there was no room for air. She gasped, panic rising in her chest, her limbs thrashing about in a desperate bid for air. Then Doña Elvira was leaning over her, gently pushing her onto her stomach and rubbing her back.

"Think of something nice," said the nurse, gently. "Think of the snowdrops and daffodils. Think of tulips and cowslips. Think of roses. You are happy here in England. Think of how you love the springtime."

Kate thought of these things and began to breathe naturally again. Then, in a flash of memory, she saw a vase of roses on a coffee table, beside a bowl of lemon drops. She saw her five-year-old self, sitting on the couch after the accident with the broken pitcher, blood dripping from her hand. In desperation and fear, she'd pulled her T-shirt over her head, trying to make a cocoon in which to curl up. But instead of creating a safe haven, she'd gotten stuck in the tight cloth, the T-shirt stretched to capacity, caught around her head and binding her arms. This was how her father had discovered her when he'd come home from work. Bound and silent, her tears worn out, terror a great dark shape behind her eyes.

Was that it? Had she equated the loss of her mother with the claustrophobia and internalized her grief as fear? Kate didn't know and she didn't care. It was enough that she had arrived at this conclusion now. It was a relief to think so, to have a reason for the fear that had seemed so irrational. As Doña Elvira rubbed her back, Kate interrogated the memories. When she had explored every detail, she felt even more at ease. Her mind drifted back to the tulips, the cowslips, the snowdrops, and she wondered sleepily if Katherine's memories of England weren't better than her own. Right now they certainly seemed easier to live with. If Kate had to live in England, maybe it would be better to remain in this time? Loss had diminished her, taken away all joy, but now Katherine's presence was rejuvenating.

She wanted to go home; at the same time, she could feel this new life tugging at her, and she thought about how easy it would be to give in, to give over to all that was Katherine. To vanish without a trace—that was exactly what she had wished for, and the wish could come true. She could make it come true.

The walls between the worlds are thinner than we think. Willow's words returned as the sound of Doña Elvira's muffled snoring told Kate that she wasn't worried her charge would wander any further tonight. And, truthfully, Kate didn't have the energy. She suddenly thought of Henry and her stomach turned in a funny, delicious sort of way. She could still feel his lips brushing hers and the warmth of his minty breath on her face. It suddenly didn't matter that she knew his future. This Henry wasn't the same one from the history books, she was sure of it. And even if he was, she could change him. She knew she could.

For a moment, Kate's thoughts turned to Hal but she pushed them away. Hal was nothing like Henry. And he was so distant now that she didn't have to think about him. Relief flowed over her even more strongly as she realized she didn't have to think about any of them—Willow, her parents, even Hal—she didn't have to think about any of them at all. The thread of possibility looped tighter, drawing her toward the idea that if she decided to stay in this place, she would be free forever from her past. And the memories from Katherine that held her here were growing stronger. As if to prove that point, as she drifted off to sleep, she remembered William's last name, one more detail in the tapestry she was putting together of her life here: it was Fitzroy.

16
The details

It was a miracle, but somehow Kate slept through the night and woke in the morning feeling deliciously refreshed. For a few dreamy seconds she tried to remember what day it was. Sunday, it was Sunday, but by the light streaming into the sitting room, she knew it was late in the morning. She'd missed chapel and Doña Elvira would be cross.

She thought for a second of Arthur and then remembered he was dead. People were always dying and you just had to accept it as part of life. Arthur had been a good person. Quiet and very young. Too young, in fact, to be a real husband to her, but she had hoped that, in time, this aspect of their lives would develop. Prince Henry's face flashed into her mind and she wondered if she would see him today. He was so handsome. And such a scholar. He would make a good leader, a good king. God be willing, she would be beside him always as his wife. She thought of her old wedding dress and wondered if the new one would be as nice. If the King gave them his blessing. She did not understand the delay; she had been suitable for Arthur, so why not Henry?

In her mind's eye, the wooden door was before her again and she stood outside, trying to hear what was going on within. The King was making his decision. Prince Henry was there with him, planning for the future. A marriage. Or not. She stood, twisting her hands in the folds of her favorite blue dress, worn on this day to bring good luck, wondering what would happen if the decision were no. And then the door opened and His Majesty came out, looking not unkindly upon her.

"It has been decided," he said, "that a visit to Fulham Palace would do you good. The sickness has been here once. We know well that it took Arthur and it may be coming again. We will protect you from it if we can. We will do everything in our power to protect you, my dear. Do not forget that." It wasn't assurance of a new marriage but it wasn't exactly discouragement. Katherine swallowed.

"Fulham Palace is not far from our embrace," the King continued gently. "A half-day's easy ride on good horses. You will be well looked after and returned to us once the sickness has passed."

"Thank you, Your Majesty," she said, her throat dry.

Kate suddenly jerked into full consciousness. What was

she thinking! These were Katherine's memories, not hers. And they weren't memories she wanted. Much as her other life had been difficult, at least she'd had some choices. Here she'd be completely powerless, waiting behind closed doors, listening for the fate that someone else would proclaim.

Yet Katherine's memories were mesmerizing. Henry, so charming, so gallant. Perhaps history could be changed. What if Kate became Henry's wife in Katherine's place? Perhaps she could ... tame him, she thought, dreamily. It mightn't be so hard a task. After all, Henry was smart. And she knew he loved her. Surely true love could conquer anything?

Kate's thoughts darted to the wolf cub and she wondered if it was safe, poor creature. She felt as Katherine felt, a Spanish princess alone in this strange country, somehow kin to the little animal. She and William could take care of it, restore the wolf to the wilds once it was strong again. Kate rolled over in bed, adrift in planning her new life. A life in Tudor England.

Then she jumped to her feet, throwing the bed covers behind her in a heap. She'd better watch out or she'd completely lose herself here in this time and forget all about going back. Saturday, 2 pm. That's when she'd left, and that's where she was headed. Saturday, 2 pm, October thirteenth, in the year two thousand and six. *I'll be home for my birthday on Monday,* thought Kate. *My real birthday*. Although there would be no one to celebrate. Willow would be busy with her stupid play. And her father ... Kate let herself slide back to the fateful day of the accident. If only she had allowed the wisdom tooth to be removed during the first visit to the specialist, they wouldn't have been on the freeway that day. Her father would have had his heart attack at home, where an ambulance might have reached him faster. But instead, she'd had to be a big baby and panic when they put the dam into her mouth, finally persuading her dad to take her home and then booking the second appointment weeks later, when she could be given medication ahead of time to calm her nerves. And so he'd died. Her fault, when she took it all apart. She felt as if tiny earthquakes were happening all over her body, as if she were cracking into a million tiny pieces.

What day was it now? Sunday, she thought defensively, trying to put herself back together. She could stay here as long as she wanted and no one could stop her, but she'd better get the facts straight. It was Sunday, but what day, what month? And, even more importantly, what year? A chambermaid interrupted her confused thoughts, tapping softly on the door before entering to remove the lantern from her room.

"I'll bring it back afore dusk, filled up with oil," said the girl. Her voice was cheery. "Did you hear about the hanging?"

Kate shook her head.

"The thief who stole the 'broidered communion cloth. He was hung at Tower Hill at dawn."

"Oh, my goodness!" exclaimed Kate, feeling sick and leaning back against the straw pillows. "Did they find the cloth?"

"No, but," said the maid, lowering her voice and crossing herself, "people said they saw him do it."

Kate thought of the girl she'd encountered in the passage, the one who'd been stealing bread. The bread had been wrapped in an embroidered cloth. Could that have been the missing communion cloth from the church? It might have been here in the palace all along! But it was too late. Someone was dead. How easily lives were taken—and over a piece of cloth!

"Cheerio!" smiled the maid, and she went out with the lantern.

"Thank you kindly," called Kate, trying to sound dignified. Her heart was beating wildly. This place was dangerous! She had to make sure nothing aroused anyone's suspicions of her, nothing at all. She must present the Katherine that all expected to see. Had she spoken of the girl in the passage, she might have saved a man's life. But what would have become of the girl to whom she'd promised mercy? And even if she had spoken in time, would people think she herself was some kind of cunning woman, and persecute her as a witch? She'd better take care. She'd just better take care or it would be her life on the line. She supposed they hung witches on Tower Hill, too.

After using the garderobe, which was an uncomfortable and smelly stone toilet in one of the bays next to their chambers, she cleaned her teeth with a bit of cloth and then ate the breakfast of bread, eggs, and figs that Doña Elvira provided. She hadn't thought she'd be hungry after eating all that peacock the previous night, but she was, in fact, ravenous.

After eating, she pinched and pulled at the garment Dona Elvira had given her to wear under her gown—a stomacher, it was called. Made of stiff, heavy fabric, it pressed inwards against her chest and stomach and made it very hard to breathe. In order to take her mind off the discomfort, she attempted to keep her spine very straight as she had noticed the other women doing. Posture is dictated by the style of dress, she remembered Willow saying. It was important to fit in here and not arouse anyone's suspicions. The long-skirted, wide-sleeved green gown was bad enough, heavy and hot, even in the cool, damp confines of the castle. Kate suddenly felt the old sensation of panic rising up, and she stood and ran to the garderobe, where she held her breath until the stomacher was torn off and stuffed into a corner under loose straw. Straw was what people here used to clean themselves, although Kate had seen a flattened wooden stick that had clearly been employed for that duty.

"You're not reading in there, are you?" called Doña Elvira. "The gong fermour's here to clean the pipes."

Hiding a grin at his title, which sounded a lot like *gong farmer,* Kate hurried out of the room and let in the grubby old codger carrying a pail and a sharpened stick. How he was going to clean the toilet she wasn't sure, but she doubted it would be any more sanitary when he was finished. With a small sigh, she went back to the sitting room, wishing that she could wear the jeans and shoes that were decidedly more comfortable but which Doña Elvira had spirited away.

As Kate sat embroidering, she began to relax, entertaining the peaceful feeling that all was right with the world. The fire was snapping in the hearth; Doña Elvira was humming as she bustled around, gathering the right thread from various sewing boxes; and maids were straightening up the bedchamber and the other rooms nearby—their humdrum chatter a soft background for Kate's needle as it darted in and out of the material she was working on. Fitting in wasn't so hard, she thought. You just had to watch and copy what others were doing, not say too much, and then, only say what you knew would be well received. Kate smiled as she threaded a needle, thinking how lucky she was that Gran had taught her a few fancy stitches.

The embroidery they were working on was a large wall hanging that depicted a pomegranate tree, the fruit hanging full and ripe and red.

"Where will you hang this when we're done?" Kate asked.

Doña Elvira looked at her sharply.

"Why, in your bedchamber, when you and Henry are bride and groom, of course. What is the matter with you?"

"I ... I—" Kate began. Maybe she wasn't so sure of herself here after all.

"You cannot refuse him," said Doña Elvira, furrowing her heavy eyebrows. "Spain depends on this match. Your duty is to marry and have children. Boy children, who will be heirs to the throne. And, God willing, Henry will be a better husband to you than Arthur was." She shook her finger at Kate and her voice rose a notch. "It has already been arranged by your parents, you know this! If you think that you're somehow better than your destiny ... I always feared that the schooling you had might spoil you. I said as much!" She had jumped to her feet and was now pacing the small room.

"Schooling spoil me?" Kate echoed.

"Women are not meant to know but to do. Even with your royal breeding, too much learning will addle the brain. Remember that and you will *do* well. Mark my words, trouble will come upon us unless you take care!" The old woman picked up a needle and then, in her haste to thread it, pricked her finger. She wrestled for a moment with the needle and thread, and then stabbed the needle back into the pincushion, looking fiercely at Kate as if she wished she, Kate, were the pincushion.

"Remember that all your blessings you owe to your husband," Doña Elvira commanded. "He is the gold coin who will shine as our sovereign. Only in your husband's absence will you demonstrate authority, while in his presence, you are as much his servant as I am. I do not know what game you think you are playing, but you have suddenly become much too independent. Be quieter, more polite, bend to his wishes. And if he wants you to kiss him, why not? What is there to lose?" She went on in an impatient mutter, twisting a skein of red embroidery silk in her hands. "Only the crown. Only our livelihood. But of these things you have no interest. You young girls, always the same."

Kate felt a cold sweat break out on the back of her neck. Fitting in here wasn't as easy as she had imagined. People's beliefs were so foreign. Women had to do as men desired, without any personal power. It was so unfair! She thought about the man Henry would become. Shaped by this culture that thought boys were superior, how could he help but grow up to be a self-serving bully? And the dominant idea that queens were supposed to produce boy children would certainly make him think his wives were to blame if sons were not forthcoming.

Maybe I can talk him into more modern ideas, mused Kate. Maybe it isn't too late—just as long as I'm careful. She shivered as she remembered the glittering look in his eye as he killed that deer, and the way he'd turned on MacQueen. Henry had a mind of his own and she didn't want to be on the wrong side of him. But if she were careful ...

"Finish it," Doña Elvira snapped, pushing the tapestry toward her. "What are you mooning about?"

"I ... well ..." gasped Kate. Then she swallowed and said through dry lips, "Actually, it's the remembering part I'm having trouble with. I ... I seem to have lost some of my memory." If she had Doña Elvira as an ally, Kate thought, maybe she could do a better job of being the Katherine everyone expected.

"What? What sorcery is here?" croaked Doña Elvira, jumping to her feet and closing the door to the hall in case any of the maids could hear. "What do you mean?"

"It's not as bad as that. I think I will be well again, and soon, thanks to your good care. But I wonder if you could tell me a few things, just so that I do not make any more errors."

"You have ... you have lost your memory!" whispered the nurse.

"Well, not all of it," said Kate. "But some. So you must fill in the gaps."

"Yes, yes, of course," said Doña Elvira breathlessly, gathering Kate's smooth hands in her gnarled ones. "What is it you wish to know?"

"Well, why was I sent to Fulham Palace? Was it to avoid the sweating sickness?"

"Oh, God in Heaven, it is worse than I feared," cried Doña Elvira, bowing and touching her forehead to Kate's knuckles. "Grant me the strength to bring her back!"

"Oh, please don't worry!" Kate said. "Just tell me the answers I require and everything will be fine. Please. I am depending on you!" She tried to will the old woman into answering her questions. After a few moments, Doña Elvira sat up, put her hands to her eyes, and then took a deep breath.

"You were sent to ... to Fulham Palace," she began brokenly, "because there was illness here, and it was feared with your poor constitution you might catch it. I had noticed that you seemed rather distraught, and I was worried about your state of mind, so I supported the journey. I thought a change might be just what you needed. Forgive me if I was wrong, if the move to Fulham created this ... this—"

"Not at all. I'm really doing much better," Kate interrupted. "Just let's finish these few questions. What will happen to me if I am not ... not well?"

"Oh, God in Heaven, what could have prepared me for this!" moaned Doña Elvira.

"Please," Kate said. "Tell me."

"Well ..." the old woman said shakily. "If you are seen to be not suitable for Henry, we will be sent back, of course. That's what will happen." Doña Elvira wrung her hands. "Not so hard for me, but for you it would be very difficult. Your father would be very angry if you were to go back."

"Back?" echoed Kate, thinking of London and then, just as suddenly, of New York, of the bed and breakfast and their old life.

"Back to Spain! Oh, Katherine, you've not forgotten Spain!"

"No," said Kate, forcing herself to speak calmly, "Of course not. But I need you to begin at the beginning, just to make sure. What place is this? And you mentioned my father, but what of my mother?"

"Why, this is the Palace of Placentia at Greenwich, of course! The court of Henry VII! And your mother, Queen Isabella, is dead, you poor, poor—" The old nurse took out a handkerchief and pressed it against her eyes.

Kate drew in a breath. Isabella. Isobel. The connection was simply too eerie to consider. She felt Katherine's pain at the death of her mother as dearly as if she herself were feeling it. But this sorrow wasn't new. This was something Princess Katherine had lived with for some time, and, as Kate explored the thoughts of the princess, she discovered comforting and happy memories blended with sad in a bittersweet mix.

"So it really gets better," she said softly, thinking about how hard it had been to deal with the feelings surrounding her own father's death. "It gets bearable."

"Oh, to have misery like this cast upon me at this stage in my life," moaned Doña Elvira. One of the maids opened the door into the sitting room and the old woman jumped to her feet, throwing off all signs of despair.

"We are without fresh water!" she announced. "Go and fill our pitchers right away. And bring a new mulberry twig for under the bed—the fleas were terrible last night."

No matter where she was, in whatever time period, Kate realized she would feel the loss of her father. But as she thought about it now, his death didn't seem to weigh upon her as heavily. In fact, as she leaned into Katherine's past, shouldering his death was easier.

Doña Elvira had begun to pace the floor, muttering to herself, and Kate caught the end of what she was saying.

"The long journey here, how we were met at the docks, and Prince Arthur's death ..." Kate desperately wrenched herself back into the conversation, hoping to find out all she could. She needed every detail that would help her find a way to survive here.

"No, really, I'm fine," Kate interrupted firmly. "Sit down please and answer the questions. I recall most things; I just want to be sure. 'Memory—' she said, remembering something her grandmother used to say, "'*—Memory depends a lot on one's perspective.*' And you have the ability to fill in a perspective I am lacking."

Doña Elvira was thus persuaded into a chair and Kate went on.

"The year is—"

"The year of our Lord, 1507," Doña Elvira obliged.

"And you are ...?"

Tears spilled from the old woman's eyes and a deep sob tore at her throat.

"I was ... I was your governess when you were small. I came with you from—" she gulped, her voice rising "—from Spain, and I will stand by you if I can, although many times over you have broken my heart. Broken it into a dozen, maybe two dozen, tiny pieces. Maybe"—here she batted at invisible shapes in the air, and her voice cracked in its sorrowful flight—"three dozen!"

This was much harder than Kate had thought it would be, and she would have gladly stopped here except that Doña Elvira continued, much like a draining tub that, once unplugged, gurgles away until empty. She filled in Katherine's past as carefully as she could, telling how the Spanish princess had been brought to England to wed Henry's sickly elder brother—fifteen-year-old Arthur—the heir to the throne.

The marriage. Kate couldn't pick up more than a bewildering train of images: flowers, a white dress, a feast set out on golden plates. Arthur, she remembered, had been such a child, really. Katherine felt almost a sisterly affection for him, as that is what they had been to each other. Brother and sister. Arthur had died six months after the wedding. Sometime after that, Katherine had been betrothed to Henry, but a month ago, the King—Henry VII—had sent her to Fulham Palace to avoid an epidemic of the sweating sickness. Doña Elvira was kept back because she was needed for midwifery—three ladies of court, including the one last night, were soon due to have babies.

"So many babies," Doña Elvira continued. "Last summer, there was trouble with other babies in Norfolk and I was kept busy all the time. Glad to leave Norwich Castle I was, when we moved along. Anne Boleyn was the last of them, the babies, and what a birth that one was ..." Doña Elvira seemed lost in thought.

"Anne Boleyn was born last summer?" Kate blurted, thinking of what Willow had told her. Anne was to be Henry's wife after Katherine.

"Ah, yes. I was called out at night and she wasn't born until noon two days later. Quite a delicate complexion but a strong breath on her."

Willow would be fascinated by such details. Kate remembered that her sister had a little notebook in which she recorded things that related to whatever play she was in at the time. A warm image of Willow, snuggled up on the couch with an afghan, jotting down information, rose up in Kate's memory but she pushed it aside, nodding as if Doña Elvira's anecdote was an event she recalled.

"I remember ..." acknowledged Kate. "The little finger on her ..."

"On her right hand! Thank goodness, you have some recollection!" exclaimed Doña Elvira.

"So Henry—our Henry—will be King Henry VIII?" Kate interrupted, her stomach tense.

"Yes, certainly," said Doña Elvira. "And a stronger king

he'll make than his brother, God rest Prince Arthur's soul. And a better husband to you."

History says differently, thought Kate. But history can be changed, I know it can! She took a deep breath, shook off the panic that was rising in her throat, and tried to remember. After Katherine of Aragon, Henry had married Anne Boleyn, whom he had put to death, and someone after that until, all in all, he'd married six women. *King Henry the eighth to six wives he was wedded: one died, one survived, two divorced, two beheaded!* But really, that was ridiculous. Henry would never hurt anyone; she, Katherine, knew that well.

"Collect yourself," Doña Elvira went on. "You must collect yourself. Soon you must meet Henry to play tennis; you arranged that yesterday and he dislikes waiting. I have slippers for you over by the bed. If you cannot remember something, hold your tongue. I shall try to come up with some herbs to assist your memory. And the leeches might help, too."

"The ... leeches?" Kate stammered.

"For bloodletting! Now go, or you will be late! And don't play too well. It is your duty to let the man win. At everything, the man always wins."

"But what happened to my old shoes?" Kate asked.

"I gave them to the grooms, of course," said the old woman. "That is who you got them from in the first place, I imagine. Although they are a sight worse than the clothing the grooms usually wear." Doña Elvira wrinkled her nose in disgust.

"Well, I need them back," Kate said.

"What? What for?" The old woman spoke sharply.

"I ... well, I brought you a present," Kate mumbled. "From Fulham Palace. I'll have to search for it, though, because I hid it in one of the old things."

"A present? What kind of foolishness is this?"

"You've been so kind to me. And so good to give me advice. I ... I just wanted to thank you," Kate improvised quickly.

The old woman's gaze softened.

"Well, I do appreciate it. Maybe I have taught you some sense after all, to compensate for that schooling, which is no doubt partly to blame for the disturbances to your mind. Will you be all right here while I go and fetch the old items?"

Kate was just about to say she'd be fine, when the maid appeared with the requested pitcher of water, accompanied by Reedy Voice who stared inquisitively at Kate.

"You two shall keep Princess Katherine company until I return," the nurse said to the maids. She bustled off, muttering to herself, "I can't imagine what she has for me; I just can't guess."

"I shall await your return," called Kate, formally. After all, what else could she do? If she bolted, the maids would be alarmed and someone would likely catch her. And then there was the threat of having her named as a witch. No, she had to be very careful.

After Doña Elvira went out, Kate put down her needle. What did she have in her pockets that could pass as a present? She thought hard because she knew she'd need Doña Elvira on her side. The maids sat and stared at her curiously. She picked up the needle again.

"'Ow are we feelin,' Luv?" asked Reedy Voice, fingering a little bundle of herbs she wore on her belt.

"Fine," said Kate curtly, staring at the dried plants.

"Thyme," the maid croaked, looking at Kate through narrowed eyes. "As an antidote, just in case!"

"An antidote for what?" asked Kate.

"Witchcraft," said Reedy Voice, picking up Doña Elvira's needle and then darting a look at the other maid who had quickly drawn her hand to her lips.

"Well, it's good to be careful," said Kate, slowly. "Nothing's bothering us in here, but you never know what you'll find when you go beyond the castle gates."

"Who says I've been ... been goin' beyond the castle gates?" asked Reedy Voice worriedly, her eyes wide. "It weren't more than thrice that I ... I went to visit—but then you must have 'eard if you're askin' me now—"

"Never mind," said Kate gently. "I didn't mean to accuse you of anything. I just meant that this castle is secure, that nothing can hurt us here."

"No, it feels quite safe in here," said the younger maid quickly. She smiled at Kate and nodded. Kate suddenly recognized her as the girl who'd been carrying the bread the other night. Maybe she was grateful that Kate had kept her secret. Now she was returning the kindness. Kate smiled in return.

"Remember that girl last July what was 'ung by the neck until she was dead?" asked Reedy Voice, conspiratorially. "She was run over by the cart in Cheapside, London, died, and then revived." She lowered her voice to a whisper. "I went to see the place but naught was there. The story is that she saw Our Lady of Barkin' liftin' the cart. And then she killed all those pigs and chickens at the local farms just by usin' the evil eye!"

"How do you know she killed the pigs and chickens?" asked Kate, and Reedy Voice looked surprised.

"Because she was a witch!" she rasped.

This circular argument didn't make sense, but Kate heeded the warning in the younger maid's expression and kept silent.

When Reedy Voice went to the window to thread the needle, Kate pushed the basket of bread on the table toward the younger maid and nodded her head. Might as well be used by someone who needs it for more than cleaning tapestries, she thought. The maid nodded gratefully and, picking up the basket, quickly left the room before Reedy Voice sat down again.

In a short while, Doña Elvira returned, carrying a bundle

that, when Kate eagerly opened it, contained her running shoes and jeans.

"Thank goodness!" she exclaimed.

Doña Elvira fastened her bird-like eyes on the clothes.

"Oh, yes, the present," said Kate.

"For me, all that I want is to see you well again," said Doña Elvira, her expectant gaze flickering back and forth between Kate and the bundle.

"Of course, but I do have this present for you," Kate repeated, digging frantically in the pockets of her jeans. The eyes of the maid bugged out at the sight of the unfamiliar clothing but she kept silent.

"Thank you for being so kind as to think of me," said Doña Elvira, folding her hands in anticipation.

Nothing was in the pockets, of course, except an old Kleenex that Kate didn't think she could pass off as a gift. She thought of the shoelaces but that didn't seem quite right, either. And then her fingers encountered something in a back pocket. It was the elastic band she'd used in her hair. She pulled it out.

"This," said Kate, "is for you."

"Oh," said Doña Elvira, staring at the object. "Well. What is it, Katherine?"

"It's ... it's a strange and magi—um, entertaining object," Kate said. She had been going to say "magical" but thought better of it. "See, you can pull it wide into a circle, and then when you let it go, it shrinks back to its original state. It represents ... um, it represents life. See, first it's the baby when it's small. You took care of me when I was a baby, remember? And then growing, growing ..." She made the elastic widen around her hands. "And then, at the end of a full life, it's small again, old bones beneath the ground. Do you like it?"

Doña Elvira's eyes were wide and the eyes of the maid were wider.

"I have never seen anything like it! Where did you get it?"

"Uh ... one of the servants at Fulham Palace gave it to me," stuttered Kate. "She makes them ... out of leather and ... and fat. Deer fat. You have to heat it," she finished lamely.

"Oh!" Doña Elvira gasped as she stretched the elastic around her wrinkled wrist. She looked at Reedy Voice, whose eyes were by now popping out of her head.

"I note we're almost out of the red yarn," said the nurse. "Please fetch some from Lady Margaret's cupboards." The maid took one last suspicious look at the elastic band and then scurried off.

"Wear it and think of me," said Kate to Doña Elvira as grandly as she could.

"Thank you, child," Doña Elvira said, looking at her kindly. Then she said, "And in your present troubles, I, too, have a gift to give. But it is a gift of advice. Believe in yourself. Just believe and your troubles will fade away."

This sounded so much like Gran that Kate felt her eyes

filling with tears. *The walls between the worlds are thinner than we think.* Willow's words returned more resonantly than ever.

"Believe," Doña Elvira repeated. "It is the power of resolution which carries us forward."

But can resolution carry me backward through five hundred years? wondered Kate, taking a deep breath. Then she went quickly into the bedroom to change, leaving the old woman marveling at the properties of the elastic band.

17
The romance

"Should I go or should I stay!" Kate muttered to herself once she was alone in her room. She wondered what might happen to the nurse if Katherine were to disappear. The death penalty? She couldn't imagine it but, in these times, anything was possible. Yet the poor woman wasn't really a jailer; she was more like a personal trainer, coaching Katherine in all things proper, responsible for fulfilling her every need.

Thoughts about Willow shifted Kate's focus. It must have been quite a burden for Willow to all of a sudden be in charge of a younger kid, like being a parent—except without the same authority. *She had the duty of carrying on while I just sat and moped.* A hot blush rose in Kate's cheeks as she thought about how hard it must have been for her sister. And where had the money come from for the private Camden school? Willow pinching pennies by serving them canned soup all the time? Gran selling her furniture? But all of that paled in comparison with her father's death. And whose fault it was. Kate closed her eyes and willed herself apart from that time. She kicked aside the slippers Doña Elvira had laid out for her and pulled on the runners. Under the gown they'd be hidden. Her feet were already covered in blisters from trying to walk in Katherine's unforgiving footwear, and today she wanted to be comfortable.

"Katherine," called Doña Elvira from the doorway. "Henry has arrived. You'll not arrange to keep him waiting."

"Uh ... no, you're right," said Kate. She went out to the sitting room where Henry stood in the doorway, looking more handsome than ever. In his hands was a strange-looking metal instrument.

"What is it?" asked Kate.

He flashed her a discerning look out of sharp blue eyes. "You've never seen one before?"

"Perhaps," she answered pleasantly. The object was round, about a foot in diameter, and shaped rather like a large compass. It had a dial that could point to one of any number of degrees etched in the metal rim, and Kate guessed the device had something to do with direction.

"It's the astrolabe," he said. "I brought it to show you as I promised I would."

"Oh, yes, the astrolabe," said Kate, looking at it curiously. She saw that the numbers etched on it increased by tens each way from zero.

Henry turned on his heel, strangely quiet, and walked down the passageway. Kate followed.

"Enjoy the tennis," called Doña Elvira. "And remember, the man always wins," she rasped.

"Here, page!" commanded Henry, beckoning to one of the young boys gathered in the great hall over a game of dice. "Take this astrolabe back to my chambers, and mind you handle it carefully. It's very precious."

As the page took it in his hands, Kate could see the child was nervous and, when he turned, he stumbled and almost fell.

"What, brat, did I not say to be careful!" Henry cried, lifting a hand as if to strike the boy. Kate stood staring, her stomach filled with anxiety at this show of power. Suddenly the jester Kate had seen at dinner appeared and stepped in between Henry and the child.

"What now, brown cow?" quipped the jester. "Is this fool not fool enough to catch your fancy? Catch as catch can, for you'll not catch me!" He jumped to one side as Henry took a swipe at him, and then scampered around the hall on three limbs, his left arm waving in the air. He was surprisingly fast, and Henry, chuckling now, was unable to catch up with him. How could Henry change from anger to good humor so quickly? Maybe Kate had imagined his intent with the page. Surely he'd never strike a little boy? Henry looked back at Kate and motioned her to follow him. The page, Kate noted, had taken advantage of the diversion and smartly made an exit.

It wasn't far to the tennis courts and the game proceeded swiftly. Henry was a good opponent. As Kate returned his serve, she couldn't help but admire his strong frame and the commanding way he moved. He was a natural athlete who had obviously taken care to hone his skills. As the play continued, she found herself energized by the recent lack of exercise and burning with the spirit of competition. In the end, in spite of Doña Elvira's advice, she won.

"Let's have another!" said Henry, his face flushed. And Kate won again.

"You are not like any other girl I know," he said, his eyes sparkling after her second victory. "I like your fire. But I will practice harder. I will be a fitting partner, you will see." He straightened his velvet jacket and came so close Kate could feel his sweet breath on her face. He reached out to touch her hand where it had been scratched and she did not draw away.

"Almost healed," he marveled. "And yet you discarded the good luck ribbon?" He looked at her anxiously. "Something is wrong. I can feel it. Please, confide in me. You are some changed, Katherine. I am beguiled but, at the same time, afraid for you."

He spoke so kindly that Kate could feel Katherine's heart responding, and perhaps her own heart, as well. Should she tell him the truth? If they were to be married, there could be no secrets. With Arthur, she had been as open as a young girl could be who had no worries. Now, though, so much depended on Henry's trust of her, his love.

"Talk to me, Katherine," he pressed. "I, of anyone, will understand."

"You ... you will?" Kate stammered, remembered affection welling up. She was sure he could see it in her eyes.

"I will," he promised, stepping forward and taking her hands in his. His fingers were smooth, warm. Kate felt her heart beating wildly.

"The problem is," Kate began, improvising as she went along, "the problem is that I did have a slight illness while at Fulham Palace." She sensed him pulling away and quickly amended, "But, of course, I'm well again now. It's just that my memory is a bit flawed. I can remember many things quite well while other things seem to escape me. In time, I believe, all will be well." She took a deep breath. He had dropped her hands and on his face was an expression she could not read.

"I knew it!" he said finally. "But, of course, I'll do anything I can to help!"

"How did you guess my secret?" asked Kate, trying to flatter him.

"Well, by the astrolabe, of course," he said a bit modestly. "It was just a little trick I played to gather some clues."

"The astrolabe?" said Kate. "I suppose I should have known more about it—"

"One would think," said Henry, "since you gave my father that astrolabe upon your arrival from Spain, you would have some recollection of it."

"That was my own astrolabe?" Kate blurted. "For shame! What a dirty trick!"

"I wouldn't be speaking so freely about tricks," said Henry stiffly.

He looked so like a cross little boy all of a sudden that Kate couldn't help but chuckle.

"There's no need to look so mad!" she admonished.

For a second, Kate thought she might have stepped over the line, but then he broke into laughter.

"Well, no harm done," he said when he had recovered his composure. "And I do believe that you are returned to health or you would not be so hardy at the tennis." He looked at her so admiringly that Kate began to soften. She supposed she could tell him the real story and see what he made of it. While she was deliberating, he came closer and spoke in a smooth, warm voice.

"There is something I have been considering for some time," he said. "And truly, I like you better than ever, for I can see the feelings you have for me. My father, the King, wanted us to proceed with caution, as he is still making decisions about a second dowry that is being offered from Spain. But marrying for love has always been part of my plan, and I fully intend to temper Father's considerations."

He leaned forward, took her chin in his hands, and kissed her. His lips tasted of mint and sage and Kate felt herself giving in to the warmth of his hands.

"Tomorrow we will play again," he said. "And I shall be a better partner."

They walked slowly back toward the palace proper, stopping every now and then to watch the sparrows that were diving down for seeds that one of the gardeners had sprinkled on the grass.

A line from a children's song kept running through Kate's head, at first comforting and then a little irritating. *His eye is on the sparrow but I know he watches me.* It was, she remembered, about God. But now it felt as if it were about her and Henry. Of course Henry would be watching her. He had to make sure that no illness could pass between them; she understood that. She tried hard to be attentive and seem well.

"And Mary, your little sister," she asked, not truly knowing whom she was talking about but relying on Katherine's intelligence. "Has she been in good spirits?"

"Yes, indeed," said Henry. "But who could not be in good spirits here at Placentia?"

Kate nodded.

"Mary reminds me of a finch," he said. "Always flitting here and there, always chirping about something."

He spoke of her so tenderly that Kate guessed he had a soft spot for his little sister. She thought back to the incident with the page and realized she must have been mistaken. This guy would never hit a kid.

"And she loves to sing," Henry continued. "Have you ever heard her?"

Kate thought for a moment but Katherine's memories came up blank.

"I don't believe I have," she said. "Does she sing well?"

"Like an angel," said Henry. "Like ... like our mother." He went quiet. Then he spoke slowly, the words pulled out one by one. "She was so young when ... when Mother died that I think she managed to remain untouched by it. A blessing, really."

Kate felt a pang, comparisons with her own mother filling her mind. She'd been only five when Isobel had vanished. And now, could she really disappear the way her mother had, without leaving a trace?

Henry went on. "Life is a pageant of loss. So one should reach for joy, I think. Reach for joy in all things."

Kate thought about this. She knew that her natural tendency was to retreat. Retreat before anything hurt you.

"How ..." she began, then stopped. He looked at her expectantly. "How does one reach for joy?" she asked, the words coming out all in a rush.

He contemplated her for a moment. "Come on, I'll show

you something," he said, catching up her hand and pulling her away from the path they were taking. They walked along the Thames, and then veered off toward a pond where Henry told Kate to stand quietly and watch. He pulled some crumbs from his pocket and tossed them on top of the water. Suddenly the surface of the pond seemed to be boiling, and Kate could see large fish making their way through the crumbs until all the bread had disappeared into hungry mouths.

"That is how to do it," he said. "These fish are wise, even in late fall when they should be slowing down. They know a good thing when they see it."

"So that's your secret to happiness," said Kate. "Eating!"

Henry laughed.

"Knowing a good thing when it comes along," he said, and took up her hand again. "Come with me!" he continued. "There is more to see!" They walked for a few minutes until they stood before a large stone tower, one open side leading into a wall of nesting boxes. Birds darted in and out, the air filled with their purring.

"Pigeons?" said Kate.

Henry gave her a surprised glance. "Doves. *Columbia livia*. Look!" He pointed up where the clouds had suddenly parted and a flock of white birds wheeled against the blue sky. "Does that not take your breath away?"

"It does!" sighed Kate, enraptured at the sight of the birds.

Without really meaning to, she leaned toward Henry and

found that he was leaning her way as well. In his arms, she felt warm and safe. And when he kissed her, her knees went weak. This guy was amazing.

On the way back, Henry asked a servant to fetch him his lute, and he played for her, the notes ringing sure and true.

"When did you learn to play?" she asked.

"I don't actually remember," he confessed. "It was so long ago. I suppose I've always loved music. It offers a voice for the heart, I think."

Kate smiled. That was a wonderful way of putting it. A voice for the heart. She tried to remember if her heart had ever really had a voice, and could not. The song he was singing to accompany the strings was captivating, and for a long time after he left her with Doña Elvira, the words ran over and over through her head:

Green groweth the holly, so doth the ivy.
Though winter blasts blow never so high,
Green groweth the holly.
As the holly groweth green
And never changeth hue,
So I am, and ever hath been,
Unto my lady true.

Green groweth the holly, so doth the ivy.
Though winter blasts blow never so high,
Green groweth the holly.

18
The promise

The next day, Henry arrived early for tennis. Kate ran to meet him, catching Doña Elvira's eye. It was not so hard, after all, to win her nurse's approval. As before, they played two games and Kate won them both.

"I do not know how you do it," laughed Henry. "But I can see that I have more practicing to do. You must have found a worthy partner at Fulham Palace."

"None as worthy as you," teased Kate. "It's just my natural talent."

"I like your strength," said Henry. "But we will play again another day and then see who is the better tennis player. Today there is another matter I ..." and here his voice faltered, "... I wish to discuss. A matter most delicate between England and Spain." He pulled a silver box from his pocket.

"I see that you are trying to hide from me your past illness because you don't wish any worries to cloud my time in your presence," he began. "It is true that sickness sometimes shadows memory, and I have seen your memory at its worst." He smiled. "But, in truth, what you remember is more important than what you have lost, and the two of us can make more memories from this moment onward. Memories, along with fine sons!" He looked at her tenderly and, when she did not reply, he continued.

"You have won more than the tennis today," he said a bit gruffly, handing her the box. Kate blinked and fumbled at the catch. When she opened the box, she caught her breath. There, inside, was a gold ring, set with a large, lustrous pearl. Henry lifted out the ring and slipped it onto her finger.

"A pearl for a promise," he said, looking at her with a man's steady gaze. "I have spoken to Father and all is well. You may give us the date. Springtime would be most suitable, two years hence."

"I ... I ..." she stuttered, feeling her face burn, "but of course I can't marry you. I might have to go back ..."

"I must confess I wasn't so sure about my brother's widow," Henry went on, ignoring her response. "I chose, along with my father, the King, that you should retire to Fulham Palace. I needed time to think. But I have made my decision. When I am King, you will be Queen."

"But I can't ..." Kate stammered. "I ... I—"

It was as if a thread were drawing Kate toward him. She couldn't say yes but she couldn't say no, either. Their hands touched again and then their lips. She felt her heart beating wildly, and then she saw his eyes glitter, just as they had when he had killed the deer, holding a look of exultation, of triumph, of finishing the hunt. She pulled back and spoke quickly.

"I can't stay!" she cried. She tried to pull off the ring but it was tight and wouldn't budge.

"Ah, but I think you can," said Henry lightly.

Kate looked at him.

"There is nothing in Spain for you now," he said. "I imagine you miss your country, but you have spent enough time here to consider this your home. Truly, your happiness means everything to me. I will do all in my power to smooth your path."

She faltered. *Reach for joy,* she thought.

"Perhaps you are right," she said. "I just ... maybe I just need a little more time."

"Time waits for no man," Henry said. "But perhaps it does wait a little for women." He grinned. "We will speak of this again. In the meantime, please wear the ring." He looked so hopeful, how could she refuse?

"I will," she said, but whether she meant wear the ring or marry him, she wasn't really sure.

There were others nearby and, rather than have their affairs out in public, Kate took his hand and they walked toward the fishpond.

"I have many people here at my bidding," Henry went on absently, as if reading her mind. "They are a necessary support for us. At times, they also make me somewhat weary. You are fortunate that Doña Elvira came with you from Spain, as childhood companions are the most trustworthy, are they not?"

Kate nodded, gratitude welling up for all the nurse had done for her.

"And we are lucky here that in our power our servants fare very well," Henry went on lightly. "They shall never come to any harm as long as they remain loyal."

Kate thought of William's father and wondered what his fate would be.

"Here, good fellow, get me a drink," Henry called out to one of the gardeners, who quickly brought him a metal cup filled with water. Henry drank it down and then held out some coins to the chap.

"Six ducats to you, then," he said to the gardener, and the man, bowing in gratitude, retreated back to his orchard.

At the gatehouse, Henry stopped and reached inside his purse, taking out a few more coins to fling at the beggars. "There," he said. "That's all I have, but come back tomorrow and I might have more."

In the courtyard, a young girl of about eleven or twelve, dressed in a bright yellow gown that looked to be made of silk, was calling in a sharp voice to a group of servants who were bustling around her.

"I said I wanted the yellow sleeves, not these white ones," she was saying. "Can't anyone find the yellow sleeves?"

"Princess Mary," began one of the ladies in waiting. "Remember, the yellow ones were left back at Norwich castle. But these white ones do look fine with your comely dress!"

"I said I wanted the yellow ones and I shall have them, one way or another!" cried the girl, and for punctuation, she sharply kicked the lady in the knee. "You must send Jane Popincourt to me—for I want to play with her—and go yourself back to the other palace for my things that were left behind."

"Here, here!" said Henry, interrupting the little scene. "What's all this over a pair of sleeves?"

"I marvel much at my brother, who doesn't keep his word about playing games, yet dares to interrupt when I am in a matter needing most serious attention!" said the child, drawing herself up to full height and looking most imperiously at Henry. He simply laughed, let go of Kate's hand, and swung the child up in his arms.

"Come for a carry, pretty Mary," he said, "and your worries will be forgotten."

Kate followed a laughing brother and sister up the stairs to one of Henry's sitting rooms, where he deposited the little girl onto a pile of cushions and resorted to tickling her mercilessly. Kate smiled as she remembered other tickling matches that she and Willow had undertaken when they were younger, and then felt suddenly melancholy.

"Truce. Truce!" Mary laughed, and finally the siblings sat side by side, contemplating Kate. "Why do you look so sad?" asked Mary. "You look as if your mother died."

Taken aback, Kate could only look at the child.

"Hush," said Henry. "You shouldn't mention that. Princess Katherine's mother died a long time ago; you've just forgotten."

"People are always dying," said Mary. "It's hard to keep track. Anyway, the others mention Mother's death to me all the time. They say, 'If only her mother hadn't died she wouldn't be so peevish.' But I'm not peevish. Can't you see, I just like my nice things all around me. Like my good yellow sleeves!" Her mouth twisted petulantly.

Kate remembered, with that uncanny store of knowledge that came from Katherine, that Mary and Henry's mother had died when Mary was not quite seven. Her heart warmed to the little girl and she looked admiringly at the golden hair.

"You have the most beautiful hair," she said honestly. "How would you like me to put it up in a French braid?"

"What's that?" asked Mary.

"Well, it's a braid that ... I learned from my ... uh ... mother, who learned it from someone else," Kate lied.

"Someone from France!"

"Yes!" agreed Kate.

"Well, all right," said Mary, tilting her head on one side to consider. "If you don't pull. I hate people who pull."

"I'll try not to," said Kate.

Henry picked up the astrolabe that the page had left on a desk, and Kate noticed how he very gently folded it in a silken cloth and then put it away in a wooden box. He saw her watching him and nodded.

"I am fond of it," he said. "I admit. At night when I feel lost, I take it out and mark our place in the universe. The stars never lie and, certainly, the sky isn't going anywhere."

"Do you often feel lost?" Kate asked quietly, brushing Mary's bright tresses with a tortoiseshell brush the child had produced from another room.

"I think of all the funerals," said Henry, an odd, tight look on his flushed face. "Sometimes I have a difficult time getting my bearings, and the astrolabe makes me feel ... makes me feel as if I could always find my way home, if I needed to. If I really were lost." Henry's voice was low and controlled but Kate could hear the emotion under his words. After a brief silence, he went on.

"Arthur's coffin, even though it was mounted on a carriage drawn by twelve horses and covered in black velvet, would, inside it, be the same as other coffins. A small dark prison, of sorts. Rather like life, at times, if you aren't careful. If you don't have ... if you don't have a way of finding your direction."

Kate watched her hands as they plaited Mary's hair. She knew exactly what Henry meant.

"Out of death, however, comes life," Henry mused. "The civil wars, for example."

That battle had lasted for over thirty years, Kate thought, surprising herself. Katherine's memories were becoming so entwined with her own that it was hard to tell which ideas were original, although if it had to do with history, Kate knew she could not take credit. In The Wars of the Roses, she mused, Henry's father had led the Lancastrian army to triumph. King Richard, the grand old Duke of York, marched his army up to the stronghold at the top of the hill and then, in a moment of madness, marched them down again to where the enemy was waiting.

The grand old Duke of York, thought Kate, the ancient nursery rhyme ringing in her ears, *he had ten thousand men. He marched them up to the top of the hill and he marched them down again.*

"When Father's army won," the Prince mused, "the house of Lancaster and the house of York were united. Just as England and Spain will be reunited."

And when they were up they were up, Kate chanted inside her head, *and when they were down they were down, and when they were only halfway up they were neither up nor down.* She felt hysterical laughter bubbling to her lips as she realized the history behind the words.

"So your mother was from the York family?" she mumbled quickly.

"Elizabeth of York was the niece of King Richard," piped Mary. "She had long yellow hair, down to her waist. And she loved to speak French, but I do not!"

"Hush, Mary, do not speak of Mother by her given name—it is not polite," said Henry, looking sternly at his sister.

"Why couldn't Father just become King without killing King Richard?" Mary asked peevishly. "He had royal blood, too!"

"Father's only a distant relative of the royal family, remember?" answered Henry. "But no one could be a stronger king than Father, so you see, in the end, he was God's choice, and it was right he took the army to defeat King Richard."

Kate thought of the story of the two little princes in the Tower, Richard's nephews, and how, if they happened to be found as adults, they would have some claim to the throne. Their story was somehow connected to William's father, accused of plotting against the King.

"I don't like armies," said Mary absently. "They make me a little bit sick. Thinking of all the killing. But I marvel much that perhaps you are right, brother. Out of death comes life."

"Edmund was the first to die," Henry continued, talking to himself now as if Kate and Mary weren't there. "And then Arthur, a year later. And then Mother, in childbirth, with the baby." He stood and walked the length of the room, lost in his thoughts, as if pondering what good could come out of all the deaths he had known.

"It was just a doll," said Mary, breaking into his soliloquy. "Not a real baby. Oww, Katherine, you're pulling!"

"Sorry," said Kate, her face hot with the mix of feelings going on inside her. Yearning. Empathy. And love.

After Kate finished the child's hair, they talked of other things and, by the time they went to the lunch table, Henry's sadness as well as Mary's sleeves were all but forgotten. The depth of Kate's feelings she contained well in a mix of casual conversation and lively questions for Mary. Her heart, however, was brimming, and she was glad to see Henry finally joking happily again with his sister. Kate watched the two of them a bit longingly. They were lucky to have each other. How hard it would be to lose a sibling, and Henry had lost three. Does Willow realize she has lost me? Kate wondered, and then pushed the thought away.

I'm better off here, she said to herself, *reaching for joy. That's my new motto!*

Women are not meant to know, but to do, Doña Elvira had told her. That was rubbish, but Kate could fit in if she kept her alternative ideas to herself. She knew with certainty that this was where she belonged..

19
The new philosophy

"Have you ever seen the dungeons?" Henry asked, after they had dined and Jane Popincourt had bribed Mary away to study her French. His tutor was indisposed and, without lessons, the Prince clearly planned to devote his entire day to Kate.

Kate wondered if he had some particular purpose in mentioning the dungeons. Perhaps that was where William's father was detained, she mused. Then she remembered that William had said, "the Tower." Were they one and the same place?

"You travel down narrow stone steps," Henry went on, "feeling the air grow cooler and damper, as if it were biting into the very marrow of your bones. Then you come to the cells, manacles attached to the stone walls to hold resisting prisoners."

Kate couldn't help but notice the boyish enthusiasm with which he spoke. The architecture of things clearly fascinated him.

"If the prisoners try to escape before we hang them," Henry continued, "we can always tie them down, although then the rats make quick work of them."

"The rats?" repeated Kate, feeling slightly sick.

"Not very humane, is it," said Henry, a bit defensively. "But we do try to make sure most of the prisoners only spend a few days in captivity—otherwise it gets quite costly."

"And then where do they go?" she asked.

"They're hanged by the neck until they are dead, of course," he said. "And it is rather useful to have them close to the court, as barren women are advised to approach the dead ones hand to hand as a way to improve fertility. Of course, Doña Elvira would have told you that?"

"Of course," said Kate.

"I imagine she has taught you a great deal," said Henry. "She is a wise woman, a cunning woman, indeed. And we will always take care of her. There will be no suggestion of witchcraft as far as Doña Elvira is concerned."

Kate kept silent. What was he getting at? she thought uneasily.

"If the prisoners are charged with treason," Henry went on, "there is the disemboweling and quartering, as well. Traitors must be severely punished as an example."

"And what if someone is imprisoned unfairly?" Kate blurted.

"The King is never wrong," Henry said firmly. "No one would be imprisoned without cause."

"But what if it were a mistake?" Kate pressed.

"The King," Henry said loudly, "does not make mistakes!" Anger flashed in his eyes, and Kate saw that she had taken a wrong turn in the conversation. Doing away with anyone accused of breaking the law was simply cheaper, whether or not the person was guilty.

"Traitors and plagues," Henry went on hotly, "are the scourge of the kingdom. And both are partners with death."

"Penicillin," Kate blurted before she could help herself.

"What?" asked Henry, startled out of his temper.

"If you had medicine to kill the virus that caused the plagues, you'd cure the illness," she muttered.

Henry studied her carefully.

"A curious notion," he said finally. "I had no idea you thought deeply about such things. I can see that we shall have a great deal to talk about."

He was smiling at her, his blue eyes clear again, and merry, and Kate, charmed, smiled in return. It was a new sensation to be speaking freely with a boy she liked. Usually she found it hard to say anything worthwhile.

"The Tower," he went on, returning to his original subject, "is for the refined prisoners who might be held for longer stays. Strong wooden grilles make fast the doorways of each of the chambers, and inside are placed a chamber pot and a stone dais that serves as the bed. White sunlight streams through the high windows, often enough to read by should occupants have book learning. There are rushes on the floor, which generally look and smell ... repulsive." He shook his head. "Unfortunately, there is little privacy."

The princes would have been miserable in the Tower, thought Kate, remembering again the nephews of Richard III who had been imprisoned there. Poor little things. Katherine's memories opened onto the whole story. Aged ten and thirteen, the boys had been a threat to the King, and, although he had overtly placed them in the Tower for their own safety, the boys had disappeared in 1483, never to be seen again.

"Edward and Richard," murmured Kate, recalling their names.

"What?" said Henry sharply.

"Edw—"

"We do not speak of them!" he interrupted.

"I ... I beg your pardon," said Kate. "I am not sure—"

"My mother was their sister," Henry said. "And she forbade us to speak of them. I won't expect to remind you of this again."

"No, of course ... of course not," said Kate. So Henry VII had married Edward and Richard's older sister, Elizabeth of

York, strengthening his right to the throne even though he'd already won the Crown in battle. The King certainly wouldn't want Richard III's nephews turning up as adults to challenge his right to the crown. That explained why he imprisoned anyone suspected of looking for them, and why William's father was being confined, although William said his father was innocent.

"A person wouldn't want to cross the Crown," said Henry. "One might end up spending a good deal of time in the Tower, or seeing a loved one there in one's place."

"Enough talk of Towers," said Kate. "I have not yet seen where the King's ale is made; let us go and have a look."

Standing, he took her arm and they left the table, going past the kitchens to the brew house. Then they strolled back to the outside rooms of the great chamber, which led to the private area where the royal family resided. Kate suddenly wondered if Henry was going to take her into his own bedroom, but he did not, nor did they go back to the study where they had been with Mary. Instead, he showed her into an elegant stateroom, where signs of the zodiac decorated the walls and gray fur pelts covered the floor. *Wolf pelts?* thought Kate.

"What shall we see next?" he asked, surveying her quizzically and then unrolling a large map that was kept in a corner. "The libraries are not generally open to women; however we could make an exception with Mother's library, as we have done before. Perhaps you'd like to stroll through one of the gardens, or we could tour the orchards? Or return to the dovecots and fishpond? The well by the pond has the sweetest water anywhere, and I have been meaning to go and see about one of the gardens, where I note William has been lingering. There must be some fruit left there if he's so keen to hang about all the time. He's been known to bribe the kitchen staff to make preserves, which somehow manage to reach his father."

"Where is his father?" asked Kate, feigning ignorance.

"Where all traitors should be," said Henry. "Except it is possible he will receive a light sentence when my father has the time to consider it."

"Will that be soon?" asked Kate, hopefully.

"Not likely," said Henry. "There is a lot of business involved in running a country. My father is extremely occupied."

Too busy to release an innocent man? thought Kate. She couldn't imagine having a father who was that busy. Her own dad had always been available, home whenever she was and always ready with a story or a joke. She thought again of the roughness of his cheek, of the woodsy scent of his aftershave, and longed to be with him. There was so much to ask, so many details of his life she hadn't explored. But of course, she would never have a second chance. Instead of allowing the sadness to fill her like an empty glass, she willed the curtain to drop, masking unpleasant thoughts. *Time to reach for joy*, she thought, and smiled at Henry.

"Does the water we drink come from another well?" Kate asked brightly, trying to distract the Prince from the idea of going out to see the garden. If he poked around the garden, he'd surely discover the wolf cub hidden there. And if the Prince saw the cub, it would surely mean its death and possibly a severe penalty for William Fitzroy.

"My goodness, you ask odd questions," said Henry. "Two wells closer to the castle serve most of our needs—however the water there tastes, I have heard, of mice."

"But the Thames is close by," Kate went on. "Why don't people just drink from it?"

"Did Arthur not talk to you about anything?" Henry asked.

Kate blushed.

"Not ... not really," she said. "We did not ... you know Arthur had a lengthy illness and even before that, he—"

Here she stopped, but Henry said, "Go on."

"Well, as you know, we were married only a few months. He was very kind. But not really a husband, if you know what I mean."

"Ah," said Henry delicately. "I had wondered about that." After a small silence, he went on. "The Thames is made putrid from the refuse flowing out of the garderobes." Kate almost laughed aloud at his change of subject, but she contained herself and listened further.

"Well water is much preferable," Henry went on, "when

one has to drink water at all. I have an idea for persuading water to climb stairs," he said, obviously pleased with himself, "and when I have a chance, I am going to build a model to see if the pressure is satisfactory. One can always improve on current practice, don't you think?" She nodded. "And surely there must be a better way to equip the toilets with some sort of constant cleaning system! Avoid the stink that carries the corrupt vapors."

"Germs aren't carried through smells but through person-to-person contact," contradicted Kate. Henry's eyes flashed.

"You don't know what you're talking about!" he said and his cheeks flushed with impending temper. "Everyone knows that foul air breeds illness due to poisonous fumes."

"I'm not wrong," Kate retorted, disregarding the warning signs. "Sickness can also be contracted by touching surfaces that have been contaminated. But it's not caught simply by breathing bad smells."

The Prince grabbed her arm.

"Stop talking about something you don't know enough about!" he said hotly.

"Maybe I know more than you think!" answered Kate.

"No girl knows as much as I do," said Henry bluntly, his mouth in a firm line. "Although I expect they wish they did."

Kate stopped herself from another retort. Henry's face was almost purple it was so red, and she could see a muscle throbbing in his neck. She was glad when the jester appeared, as if by magic, to break the tension. Even Kate offered a faint smile at the motley attire of the fellow—brightly colored patchwork clothes with bells tied around the knees, and a horned hat.

"Sir, what say ye with your fat face?" quipped the Fool.

The line of Henry's mouth hardened even further and Kate wondered if he were going to fight this bold clown. Then the prince grinned and it appeared the storm had passed.

"Have you forgotten it's ale tasting day, your royal head? Chase me down the stairs and I'll ask you a riddle."

"Tournament day? I had forgotten!" said Henry delightedly. "What's the riddle, Patch? Tell me now for I'll not be forestalled."

"What walks on no legs at dawn, then four legs at noon, two legs at dusk, and then finally back to none at night?" cried the fellow, swinging something on a pointed stick that Kate thought looked suspiciously like the internal organ of some deceased animal.

"Hmm, let me think," said the Prince.

"Man," said Kate. Her father had told her this one and she'd had to work out that the description referred to a baby, then a crawling child, an adult, and finally an old person in bed. Patch shot her a wary look, and Henry paused for just a moment before nodding rather sheepishly.

"A point for Katherine, surely. But now we must prepare for the tournament! Patch, please walk the princess back to her chambers, for I have things to do!" Without waiting for a reply, Henry strode off, and the Fool looked blandly at Kate.

"Come along then," he sang. "One, two, nine!"

Running ahead of her, he executed three back flips and then walked on his hands until they'd reached the door to her rooms. One of the maids, scurrying about with linens, laughed uproariously at the sight of Patch.

"Everyone come and look!" she cried. "'Is arms and legs 'ave changed places!" Other servants ran over to share the fun.

Flipping right way up, the jester bowed low to all the ladies and then scurried off down the corridor.

"Patch!" called a young voice. "Come here! I want you to play mumchance with me!" It was Princess Mary.

Kate knew how to play this game. You shuffled the cards and then laid the pack face down. Each player called out the name of a card and you took turns turning cards over until that card was exposed, earning a point for the first to have predicted it. Then you began again and the game was over when someone reached ten points.

"It isn't fair!" she heard Mary cry. "Patch won't play with me! No one wants to play with me!"

Kate called after her, "Princess, come here and I'll play the game." The golden-haired child appeared, smiling again, and the two of them sat over cards by the fire for an hour or so. Doña Elvira watched with a curious expression, and Kate wondered if Katherine had played much with Mary. Kate's heart went out to the lonely little girl. No mother, a father occupied with foreign affairs, an older brother too busy to play, and an older sister already married off to a Scottish King who was sixteen years older than she was! What did life have in store for this child? Kate wished she had paid more attention in history class.

"I have to use the garderobe," said Mary after a while. She skipped off and Kate looked at the fire burning in the grate. She didn't want to think about those toilets, smelly as they were in spite of the green cloth that covered the stone holes until removed by the user. Henry's plans to make the facilities more sanitary would come none too soon.

The sound of festivities outside brought Doña Elvira to Kate's side. "We shall be attending," said the nurse. "Dress in something finer than that old blue gown. Or at least wear one of your good cloaks. The one with the nice miniver lining."

"I'm going to go and change," announced Mary, dancing back into the room. "I always wear my best things to tournaments. But I don't have the yellow sleeves. How can I go without my good sleeves?" Her voice rose to a loud wail and Kate knew she had to act quickly.

"Your white sleeves are better because they won't distract the horses. Horses always look at yellow, and the riders might not go as fast if the horses are always looking your way."

"Really?" asked Mary, considering.

"Really!" said Kate. "Just like bulls always go after red."

"I marvel much at that," said Mary slowly. "I had heard about the bulls, of course. But the horses. That's something new."

"Come see my nice cloak," Kate went on, pulling the younger girl toward her closet. "So soft and warm, you'll never guess what it is made of." She herself didn't know what miniver was, but no matter—the girl was already stroking the soft fur.

"It would take a lot of squirrels to make this," said Mary. "How many, do you think? A hundred? Two hundred?"

"A hundred and fifty," said Kate, gently guiding Mary toward the passage. "Come on, we don't want to be late." Doña Elvira followed and when they got outside, the old nurse told Mary all about what they were going to see.

It's handy to have a child around, thought Kate. *People explain things to children, and that can be useful!* Her head was spinning with all the new information as she prepared to watch the fair. It didn't sound particularly fun but, in spite of her predictions, the day turned out to be interesting. First, they watched the jousting. Heralded by trumpeteers announcing the beginning of the match, two armored knights rode against each other and used their lances to try and dismount their opponent.

Kate's complete attention was drawn by a fellow in red

and black. He was graceful and quick, broke numerous lances as onlookers cheered, and earned many points by dislodging riders. When at the end, he removed his helmet to receive the first-prize ribbon, she saw with surprise Henry's flaming red hair. He turned and gave her a wave, which she self-consciously returned.

"Tsk, tsk, I thought his father, the King, did not allow him at the joust," said Doña Elvira disparagingly. "Well, young people these days have not the same respect for their elders that once was had, that is certain."

Eating and drinking went on all day. There were jugglers, acrobats, jesters, and minstrels, and Kate was impressed at their dexterity and skill. One musician in particular caught her eye, as he looked and carried himself a lot like Henry. Perhaps the two were somehow related. She gazed around for William but did not see him.

The Prince located her a couple of times to retell his triumphs and make sure she was watching his progress through the events. "This temporary seating is inadequate," he said, looking at the wooden planks on which she sat. "When I am King, I shall build a permanent tiltyard here, overlooked by a viewing gallery." Kate merely smiled and drew her cloak more tightly around her shoulders. A young page, bearing away Henry's ribbons, dropped the handful on the ground.

"Clumsy oaf!" cried Henry, cuffing him on the ear so hard that the lad toppled and fell. "Take better care or you will find yourself in the stocks!" The boy scrambled to his feet, holding his hand to his head and mumbled apologies that Henry did not acknowledge.

Kate saw fear on the child's face as well as hurt, and she frowned. *The little boy should have been more careful,* she thought. *That is, after all, his job. To be careful. Better he learn that sooner rather than later, when the stakes are higher. Still ... he is just a lad.* She noticed how skinny and pale his arms were as he picked himself up and stumbled away.

By nightfall, she was exhausted and hoped for nothing more than sleep. Instead, she had to undergo the bath, an embarrassing ordeal as there was absolutely no privacy. Servants brought in a large wooden bathtub and set it by the fire. It was filled with hot water carried in buckets and poured on top of the white sheets that Doña Elvira had used to line the tub. Finally, scented salts were poured in, and then Kate was told to disrobe in front of them all and enter the water. When she pointedly looked around at the maids bustling about, Doña Elvira simply clicked her tongue. "Get on with it!" she said, sharply. "You looked quite pale today. The warm water will do your complexion good."

The worst came when she'd gotten settled in the hot water and Doña Elvira shuffled over with a pail. She used a long handled wooden spoon to fish out a slimy looking black lump which she deposited on Kate's right arm.

"Ugh!" cried Kate. "What is that!"

"Hush!" admonished the nurse. "A leech, of course. We'll just use two tonight." By this time, a second lump was expanding near the first.

Kate felt the eyes of the maids on her and stifled a scream. She turned her head and splashed a little with her free hand, trying not to think about the activity on her arm. When Doña Elvira thought the leeches had taken enough blood, she used a thin piece of wood to scrape them off. Then back into the pail they went.

"Now," said the nurse. "We'll scrub your hair and you'll be done!"

Kate lay in the lukewarm water, trying not to think about anything. She realized she was hungry, and what rose up in her mind was a visit to London's West End when she and Willow had spent an afternoon at Covent Garden, going through shops and listening to street performers. London was really quite exciting when you gave it a chance. She had admired a little heart necklace and Willow had bought it for her. The trip had culminated with the purchase of two jacket potatoes, hot inside their foil and topped with sour cream, onions, bacon, and mushrooms. Kate's mouth watered, thinking about how good hers had tasted. She suddenly realized that they didn't ever have potatoes here.

When at last Kate gratefully escaped to her bedroom, she was so tired she could barely stand. Wearing only the white shift she had been given in which to sleep, she leaned heavily against the side of the bed.

"I'll take away the filthy gown!" said Doña Elvira, bustling in and listing tasks for the coming day. "That blue dress needs a good boiling and a mend at the hem. Now get some sleep, like a good girl."

Kate did as she was bidden, climbing under the covers with a deep sigh. There was something she wanted to think about more, something to do with Henry, but it would have to wait. Darkness reached up to claim her and she sank reluctantly into its arms.

20
William

It was just before dawn on Monday morning when William opened the door of the shed and contemplated its inhabitant. The cub's wail of desperation confirmed his fears. He knew the cub was very hungry and quickly put down a store of food. Yesterday's festivities had gone on for so long with so many people about that he had not been able to safely attend to the poor creature.

"There, there," William said, stroking its back, then slapping at his arm as a couple of fleas hopped towards him from the spiky gray fur. "You were cooped up all day yesterday and I know it isn't easy." He wrinkled his nose at the smell of the place. The straw here was rank and there was no way to clean it without drawing attention to the occupant.

"I'd rather be tied to a tree and pelted with hazelnuts than abide in this stinking shed," muttered William.

Although the cub didn't know what was said, the calm, hopeful tone of William's words was relaxing. It ate quickly, but as soon as the food was gone, another kind of hunger set in, a hunger for fresh air and sunshine. Another desolate wail escaped from its throat. William wondered if he had done the right thing in taking the cub out of the wild. When he'd found it in the marsh, he'd been off on one of his wanders, lonely for his family and trying to think of a plan to help his father. The cub had looked so piteous that William had acted impulsively, scooping it up in his jacket and conducting what he'd envisioned to be a heroic rescue. But now he wondered what he had rescued the cub for. Surely a quick death would have been preferable to an agonizing imprisonment here.

"What we need to do," he began, softly, "is find you another place to live. Somewhere closer to the forest, so you'll have some opportunity to learn to hunt. Unless you can fend for yourself, life will be terribly difficult for you." *But finding you another place,* he thought, *will be terribly difficult for me.*

The food was now gone and the cub nosed around half-heartedly in case something had been missed, but only half-heartedly.

"I suppose we have to try," William said, giving the cub one last pat. An idea rose in his mind that seemed plausible. Not perfect but it had possibilities. "There's another place on the other side of the chapel and it would give you a little more room," he said. "Plus it's closer to the woods, and we could plan some hunting when you're ready. Better than only bread for a growing animal. Sound all right to you?"

Able to translate the excitement in William's voice, the cub stood in anticipation.

William produced a length of rope that he tied securely about the cub's neck. "You'll need to wear this, for if you got away on me now, the dogs would have you for sure. Stay close, and be as quiet as you can."

As they left the hut, the young man took a deep breath. How good it was to breathe the apple-scented air, to stand in dawn's first light. He said a quiet prayer of thanks and then led his charge down the path and up the road, steering it away from the water. The animal sniffed, pulling eagerly toward the river where there would be minnows in the shallows and water birds. But William was insistent.

"This way," he said. "Come on, quickly now, before we're discovered."

They crossed a great garden, moving stealthily among the rows of fruit trees and old raspberry canes that seemed to shimmer in the early morning mist.

"Almost there, lad," said William. "Just a little further."

But it was a long time before they reached their destination, and the cub had to limp a great distance along a wide road with stones that William knew were bruising the tender pads of its feet. It was with relief that they turned through a green meadow where the going was gentler. At last they stood in front of a rickety shed, a door leading from one side to an outdoor area that was fenced from all angles.

"An old chicken coop," said William, as if the animal could understand, guiding it around to the front where a crooked door hung from rusty hinges. The ancient wood had been punished by rain and sun, and there was little sign of the paint that had once transformed the slats from brown to white. The walls were no doubt standing because the nails had been hammered and then flattened inside to prevent removal, giving them extra strength. His father had taught him all about doornails. He smiled again, thinking of Mary's phrase, *dead as a doornail,* and suddenly understanding the analogy. The nails, bent out of shape, could never be used again, and so were fully and completely dead.

"There used to be a farm here before it burned with the forest," he explained to the cub. "All that's left is this coop but it'll do for our purposes. You'll have an indoor area for shelter, in case someone comes, and an outdoor spot where you can catch the breeze. When you're stronger, the woods aren't far and, in a few days, perhaps we can try them out. I hope you are in agreement?"

The cub responded to the lilt of William's words and gratefully dragged itself inside the coop and lay down on the straw, a long sigh escaping as William slipped the rope from its neck.

"That's it, make yourself at home!" he said, busying himself with pouring water from his flask into a dish that stood in a length of thin sunlight. The cub wrinkled its nose at the acrid smell of bird flesh that wafted up from long ago, and then closed its eyes.

William stood for a moment, watching the cub sleep. It was a miracle it had survived, and it would be another miracle if it learned to hunt and take care of itself, but William knew that a life in captivity was no life at all for one such as this. Was no life for anyone, really. He thought of his father, curled up on a pallet of straw, or perhaps without comfort on a hard wooden frame, shivering in the damp. A wave of helplessness washed over him.

"I'm trying," he muttered brokenly to himself. "I'm trying as hard as I can."

Turning, he went out of the coop and closed the door behind him, locking it from the outside with a wooden latch. Then he started back toward the castle, rubbing at hot tears that burned his cheeks. Crying was no use. If only he were a powerful man with influence. Waiting for Henry to intercede on Father's behalf was like waiting for a miracle.

"But miracles do happen," William whispered, brushing the sandy hair from his eyes and trying to bolster his courage. "Miracles do happen, and, God willing, they might happen here."

21
The friendship

Days coasted by on the ragged October wind whose chill kept Kate indoors much of the time. She was able to steal away after Chapel, on occasion, to see the wolf cub, but a trip to the stables, considerably farther, did not easily materialize. Her thoughts of home seemed windblown as well—and she sank deeper and deeper into the richness of living each day in the moment.

To everything there is a season, she thought one day as she picked at her sewing—or were these Katherine's thoughts? *To everything there is a season, and a time to every purpose under heaven.* She remembered with sudden clarity her father saying these lines, the rich timbre of his voice, his smiling eyes. *Dad,* she thought, with a longing that she'd nearly forgotten, a surge of memories threatening to break free. And then, as one might close a book, she stopped the tide, turned her back on the ocean of thoughts in which she knew she'd drown. Reaching for the sewing basket, she deliberated: *Which red would be best ...*

Henry was compulsively busy, hawking, hunting, or working on various activities within the palace with which he insisted Kate assist him. It was clear that everyone admired the Prince, and, wherever he went, praise for his accomplishments rang loud and long. *No wonder,* thought Kate, in one of her few quiet moments, *that he thought so much of himself. Everyone else so obviously does, or has to say so.*

Yet, indeed, there was much for Henry to be proud of. He did have a bit of a temper, but if Kate were careful, she could manage to let sleeping dogs lie. Henry was creative and inventive, and while Kate doubted his experiments with mechanics would lead to the motor car, she was sure his designs for innovative plumbing were quite functional. He had plans for new weapons, and his passion for astronomy was admirable, along with elaborate maps he had devised of heaven and earth. The Prince confided one day to Kate that even though Martin Waldseemuller had recently published a new world map, naming in honor of Amerigo Vespucci the continent of America, his own maps would one day grace the world stage.

Kate wondered at her own lack of skills. What had she been doing all these years? Skipping school came first to mind, but she concluded that her whole life had seemed bent on avoidance. Had she really been pushing life away, as Willow had accused, securing herself where she imagined nothing could touch her? There seemed to be so much to learn, and time, as Henry said, waited for no one.

The desire to see Willow again had diminished into a faint hope that was easy to set aside. Kate wondered occasionally about how things were back home, but her memories had become as thin as the winter sunlight that left faint warmth on her skin. Indeed, it was truly as if this had always been her real life, and that other life the dream.

She was aware of time passing, but complacent. In the few stolen moments when she encountered William at the side of the wolf cub, she enjoyed hearing his stories of rural life, piecing together information about life outside the palace, the details of which even Katherine was ignorant. William knew a great deal about sheep farming and Kate asked many questions. In the spring, it was he who had cared for any orphan lambs on the family farm. He would at first tempt them with a moistened cloth, then slowly lower the cloth to the surface of a pail of milk so that they would learn how to drink. When the lambs were ten days old, he would introduce them to tender grains.

"You should see them jump," he laughed one day, speaking of the young lambs. "They run forward, then leap into the air with such lightness of being. At times I used to think them airborne creatures, just waiting for the right wind to set them on their course. Would that we all had such joy in motion."

"Don't you find it hard to butcher them, when the time comes?" asked Kate.

"No," said William, without a moment's hesitation. "They have had what is, for them, a good life. No matter how long it lasts. That is the best any of us can wish for—to make use of the time we have. To fill our place. To create joy for others. That is our calling."

Kate, at the time, disregarded his words, but later they returned to her again and again. *To create joy for others.* A different take on life than the idea of simply reaching for joy. Perhaps a richer take, she thought, but more difficult. How could she create something for others when she had known so little of it herself?

Yet Henry seemed to be working hard to even the score. He brought her poems and many little notes expressing his delight with her, each visit seeming even more pleasant than the last. Days passed, then weeks. Occasionally Kate recollected how Henry had cuffed the young page, and she soon had other similar incidents to compare, but these thoughts were not entertained for long. Henry did have a bad temper but you just had to stay on his good side, and Kate got quite competent at doing just that.

Kate wondered vaguely one Saturday, if it was still Saturday at 2 PM back home, or if it was already into November, as it was here. Whenever she asked exactly what day it was,

Doña Elvira snapped that it was the day after yesterday and that Kate should start paying attention. She knew with some certainty that she had been here over a month, that the year was 1507, and that fall had shifted fully into winter with weather dark and depressing. The passage of time was less important, somehow, when one was living each day for its best moments.

Her constant comfort was the hours she spent in the library on the Queen's side, a room unused by most of the palace but which contained a long shelf of books—more books in one place than Kate had seen anywhere else here in Tudor times. Many of the books contained religious content written in an English she found difficult to comprehend, but the inscriptions were fascinating. *To my Little Jewel, from Grandmother Neville; This book I give to my Treasured Daughter; To my Little Niece, Ever yours, Uncle Richard.* In contrast to the latter note, she found a book of love poems inscribed *To my Own Dear Darling, Your Richard.* Were these Richards one and the same? Had King Richard ever been romantically inclined toward his youthful niece? Yuck, thought Kate. That's not even legal! Then there were other books that read, *To an Intelligent Reader, Your Faithful Servant, Sanctorius; To my own dear Wife; To my Dear Daughter-In-Law, with kind regards, Lady Margaret.* This latter was a glossy collection of Bible verses in Latin alongside their English translations. Another title given to Elizabeth from her mother-in-law and lavishly illustrated was a *Book of Hours*, published in 1494. Like many of the books on the shelf, it contained tiny annotations along the inside margins—the sign of a studious reader, thought Kate. Henry's mother was more than just a pretty face. She'd clearly had an intellect to be reckoned with.

Kate's favorite titles turned out to be a series of stories about Robin Hood, whom she gathered must have been a real fellow and a hero even in this century. These were boldly illustrated with crude black-and-white prints, although some included very complicated cross-hatching, where sections were shaded in with numerous fine lines. The stories were refreshing, taking her out of the day-to-day world, if only temporarily.

"I hope Mother is working with Charlotte on her sums," William said one evening as they shared a companionable hour in the library. He had begun to join Kate there when the days began to shorten, and Kate sensed in him a loneliness that grew with each passing week.

"Is that how you learned?" Kate asked. "At your mother's knee?"

"No, I went to school in the village," reported William. "But that won't do for Charlotte as she is a girl."

"So girls' learning is less important?" asked Kate.

"No, not necessarily. It's just done differently," answered William. "Father would have seen to it had he been home. Or Mother, were she not so busy. But now I fear poor Charlotte will much be going without."

"Stop scratching!" Kate said, frowning at him. "Pour on a little vinegar to ease the itch." She had never known anyone as susceptible as William to flea bites. Hard to believe he'd lived on a farm for most of his life.

"Didn't you have fleas back home?" she asked.

"They didn't bother me as much," said William. "Maybe they preferred the animals and stayed off the people."

"Is life here in court very different from what you were used to?" Kate probed.

"Court life is indeed different from real life," said William. "In my family, both my parents have equal responsibility for the farm, unlike court where it seems as if the duties of men and women are altogether separate. A good thing, too, that my mother has such skills, for she manages much during my father's absence."

"And your brothers and sisters?" Kate asked.

"The two eldest brothers work the land and a third manages the sheep," William answered. "It isn't easy without Father. If I were there, I'd help with the lambs, but I did not have much choice in the matter. When you're called to court, you must seriously consider the offer."

"Would you rather farm, then, than study with the Prince?" asked Kate.

"I do appreciate most of my studies," responded William. "And, God willing, this learning may help me in my dream of writing a ... a book. A book about general farming." He dug furtively at a spot on his side, the color rising in his cheeks.

"A book?" Kate heard the surprise in her voice.

"And why not?" he replied, a little defiantly. "Just because the technology is new, there's no reason to think common people should not have access."

"Oh, of course," Kate said quickly. "Like tractors and stuff, right?"

"Tractors? What are you talking about?" said William.

"Oh, I thought—when you said technology ..." she stumbled.

"The technology of printing. The printing press. Have you not heard of it?" he asked more kindly.

"Oh, I see! Of course," said Kate. "I understand you now. That is a ... a wonderful idea."

"People have no way of getting information about farming without literature," said William. "Only wealthy gentlemen can travel and, other than gossip at inns and alehouses and watching closely the activities of one's neighbors, the spread of ideas about good practice is slow, indeed. Of course, we need to have more people learning to read, but I believe that practices are changing. Since Gutenberg's invention of the printing press, more people have access to written texts, and the desire to learn to read has thus increased."

"And what exactly would you include in such a book?" Kate pressed him.

"Well, I had an idea some years ago that my father took seriously. There were a lot of lambs in our flock each spring and not enough fresh grass for feed. I said it would be good if we could somehow bring river water over the grassland all winter, keeping the soil warm as water does, and then drain it off in the spring so there would be an early lush crop of grass on solid ground."

"And that worked?" asked Kate.

"It did, indeed," said William. "Father found a way to channel the water just as I'd suggested, and we were able to feed our lambs and sell them at the market before most other lambs were ready. In fact, in his last year at home, my father made a trip to Eastcheap, one of London's premier meat markets, where he was well rewarded. This and other ideas I have ready for publication when the time comes."

"So, couldn't you just write the book now?" Kate asked.

"First I must attend university, which I hope to do as a student who receives a free education by serving at table. Once I have a degree, I believe I would be in a better position to write. However, if my mother needs me at home when I am allowed to leave this place, I will heed her wishes."

"Your mother must really miss your father," Kate said.

"They were inseparable," said William. "I used to hear them talking well into the night, planning family activities, laughing together about some small joke. They were true partners in every sense of the phrase."

His words made Kate think fuzzily of the couple on the train, the businessman and the Goth. Two people so different and yet so in tune with each other. The recollection was blurred, almost as if she had imagined it. Much of the time spent in London and before had become hazy, as if those memories were covered with a cottony cloth that let light through but not much else. She sighed and thought of Henry. How she longed for more of the closeness she felt when they were together. Henry's attention was constant, but he was so busy with his tutor and his father's lessons in politics that he did not have a great deal of free time.

"Mother lives for Father's return, and the hope of returning to her is what keeps Father alive in prison." William brushed his hand across his eyes and then picked at the flea bites along his arm. "So far, I have not been much use to them. But I hope that soon the King will authorize a pardon. I must just keep trying to plead Father's case with the Prince." Kate and William sat for a short while in silence, each thinking of goals that lay unrealized. When they resumed their reading, Kate gratefully welcomed the chance to put aside heavy thoughts. You couldn't be anxious all the time!

As time went on, Kate slipped further and further into the routines of day to day, lulled into the rhythms and expectations of life at court. Although she could separate Katherine's sentiments from her own if she tried, she generally stopped distinguishing one from another. It was easier to act as one person. The only secret she studiously kept from Henry was the existence of the wolf cub. She and William took charge of the animal, their unspoken agreement to silence covering more than just the wolf cub's care. It wasn't suitable to be seen in each other's company, especially as Kate was engaged to the Prince, and both of them knew it.

As they waited one day for the wolf to finish a romp in the woods, Kate found herself telling William about missing her mother. "The way she left us, so suddenly, was the worst of it," she said.

"I've heard that royalty have many expectations placed upon them," said William gently. "Perhaps your mother wanted to be with you but it just wasn't possible. And death, you know, comes someday for us all."

She didn't die, Kate thought, but then Katherine's memories flooded her mind. Isabella had died, and quite suddenly. But Isobel—the confusing juxtaposition of two mothers gave Kate a headache and she tried to drop the subject.

"Perhaps," she said. But she remained unconvinced and unforgiving.

"I'm sure my little brothers feel I've deserted them," William went on. "We used to play all sorts of games. The youngest, Fred, was only three when I left. Dear little Freddy. I'd pull him on a sack around the yard and he'd crow with joy. And Richard, just beginning to learn his sums. How I miss them. After breakfast, my mother would gather the little ones and say, 'Now, what must you NOT do?' and they would recite their previous exploits so earnestly. I recall when a particular chasing game was in high favor, and somehow they had tumbled down on a neighbor come to tea. The next morning, they replied to mother, 'We must not run down Lady Whittington.' My older brothers and I rocked with laughter at that."

"How many brothers do you have?" asked Kate.

"Six. Five living. I once had three sisters but two have already gone with the angels, leaving only Charlotte. She is four years younger than I am and very keen on her studies. We had hoped that Father would be able to tutor her as he did the boys before they went to school, but prison has prevented that dream from coming true."

"So you come from a family of ten children," said Kate.

"Yes. And you?" asked William. For a moment, Kate couldn't remember. Then she answered, "Six. Joanna and Maria are my only living siblings." She smiled at William. "Isn't that silly? For a moment, I couldn't think of their names. I am the youngest."

"Do you miss them?" he asked.

"*To everything there is a season,*" said Kate, copying her father with surprising ease. "As Queen, I will be Ambassador to Spain and have much work ahead of me. I do hope I will see them, Maria especially, but I am not counting on it. My life is here."

William gave her a look she could not read, and the gaze from his brown eyes remained soft and questioning.

"I do miss my dog, a spaniel," she continued. "He was to come to England with me, but just before we sailed he disappeared. He was a lovely black and white creature with long silky fur, and such a good listener."

"I also grew up with a dog," said William, looking down at his hands. "Rover."

"You call your dog Rover?" asked Kate, chuckling that anyone would give an animal such a common name.

"Why, yes. What's so funny about that?" asked William, as she laughed harder. "Actually, *called* would be more appropriate. He died a few weeks after I arrived here."

Kate sobered instantly.

"I'm so sorry," she said, touching his arm.

"So maybe your mother couldn't help it," William repeated, his plain and honest face gentle and concerned. "My next eldest brother and two younger sisters were taken by the fever. I am sure it was not in their minds to leave us, as it was not in Rover's, but, indeed, they were all called to a greater good." He scratched at his arms until Kate gave him a warning look.

"I don't know if she could help it or not," said Kate. Then she sighed. "I just remember waiting for her and then for my father all one afternoon, my hand bleeding from a cut I'd gotten on some broken glass. I can't help wondering if her leaving was all my fault." Then Kate thought about her father's death. That had been her fault, too.

"Is that how you got this scar?" asked William, carefully turning over her left hand to display its palm.

"Yes," said Kate, her skin tingling strangely at his touch.

"K for Katherine?" he asked, smiling a little.

"K for ... Kate," she said, startling herself at this revelation. Where had it come from?

"Ah, Kate. A noble name," he said, reaching out and formally shaking her other hand. "Of course, you know that none of it was your fault," he went on gently, returning the hands to their owner. "To everything there is a season ... a time to be born and a time to die. We cannot control the fates any more than we can prevent them. Rest easily. It was not your fault."

Kate looked at him, feeling as if pent-up darkness were draining away until all that was left was a heady sensation of light.

"Do you ... do you really think so?" she asked, knowing the answer even before he nodded.

"K for Kate, we had best be getting back to the castle," he said, drawing her to her feet. "The sun is on its downward slide."

She stood and leaned on his arm, wobbly for a moment, happiness enveloping her like a warm wind. They saw the wolf safely back indoors and William whispered into the darkness of the shed: "Soon. Soon, you'll be free."

With freedom comes danger, Kate thought, steady again. Was it a chance that was worth taking?

22
Sanctorius

One day not long after that, following a hearty breakfast of porridge and cream, Doña Elvira dragged Kate off to see Sanctorius, a very tall, very thin man with a smooth chin and a bushy white handlebar moustache, who spent long hours as the royal accomplished natural philosopher in one of the castle's larger chambers. Kate remembered seeing his name inside a book belonging to Henry's mother. Perhaps while she was alive, the Queen had provided him with money for his experiments, thought Kate, and he had given her that book as a gift of thanks.

While Doña Elvira was secretively telling Sanctorius Kate's problems, namely limited memory, which she attributed to tiredness of the brain, Kate cast about the room, noting a long table with various unfamiliar items. Among the mysteries laid out there stood an old-fashioned weigh scale and a dozen jars full of things that resembled prunes. Soon Kate realized that these were leeches.

She quickly strode past the table and over to the bookshelf, where she poked into various large volumes, all of which had the name *Theophrastus Bombastus von Santorio* on the inside cover. The name brought a smile to her face and, after a while, she couldn't resist asking in the most polite manner who Theophrastus Bombastus von Santorio was.

Sanctorius got rather flustered and said that it was none of her business what any of his previous names were, or the reasons he had decided upon his new name, as he was such a very accomplished scientist that the matter of a name was none of her concern.

"Women of good breeding," Doña Elvira informed her, "do not ask impertinent questions." She turned to Sanctorius, a name Kate thought more feeble than the very jolly Theophrastus, and said, conspiratorially, "You see what I mean about her? Is this not a sign of an overactive brain?"

"Well, it's possible," he said, stroking his non-existent beard. "Very possible. However, not to worry—I have the solution for this young lady."

He went over to a table and picked up a small bottle filled with murky-looking liquid.

"A glass dropperful of this tincture once a day should do the trick," he said soulfully. "Should have her returned to health post haste."

"What is it?" Kate asked, remembering the headache she'd had from the drink Doña Elvira had given her and the concoction of powdered sapphires for the pregnant maid.

"Well, you see, my dear girl, what you have is an imbalance of the humors."

"What?" asked Kate.

Doña Elvira shook her head and frowned.

"Do not be impudent!" admonished the nurse.

"The world has many marvels to discover—do not disparage her questions," Sanctorius responded. Then he drew himself up to his full height of six-foot-five and leaned toward Kate.

"This may be a trifle difficult for you to understand, my dear, but I shall put it in simple language. You see, the body is a chemical system, primarily involving salt, sulfur, and mercury. Each illness caused by a chemical imbalance can be treated by adding the correct counterbalance to the body. Such is what I have in this bottle for you!"

He flourished the bottle at Kate.

"But what exactly is in the bottle?" Kate asked, burning at his condescension.

"Listen carefully," he said, speaking as if to a young child. "An outside force has entered your body and left an archeus, which is growing bigger every day and depleting your body of chemicals."

"An archeus?" Kate asked, thinking suddenly of the power

of love. Was love such a force? Thoughts of Henry filled her head and she went weak in the knees.

"An archeus is like a seed. In your case, the chemical inside the seed is depleting your body of iron. You feel tired, lethargic, and it is hard to make your mind work properly. Do not fear. This element will do the trick." He enthusiastically shook the bottle.

"But what is it?" Kate asked. "What is the element?"

"Well, but it is elementary," said Sanctorius. "Mars is associated with your ailment because it has the characteristics you so desire—strength, integrity, and clarity of thought. Since Mars is associated with iron, we must give you iron to counterbalance the ill effects you are experiencing." He delicately placed the bottle in Kate's hands.

"There's iron in this bottle?" Kate said, gingerly smelling its contents.

"But of course," smiled Sanctorius, nodding at Doña Elvira. "See that she takes one dropperful in the morning and two at night."

"I thought you said just one dropperful a day!" exclaimed Kate.

"I determined as a result of our most recent conversation that you need three dropperfuls," he amended, with somewhat less of a smile. "Now, if you ladies will excuse me, I am very busy. I must hurry and weigh my lunch because soon it will be dinnertime."

Doña Elvira had picked up the jar of leeches and Sanctorius nodded.

"Just exactly what I was thinking," he said, nodding at Kate. "At bedtime, of course. Say ... for three nights."

On the way down the stairs, Kate asked Doña Elvira what kind of experiment Sanctorius was doing with the weigh scale.

"He's comparing the weight of what he eats to, you know ... ah ... his excrement," she said, batting her eyelashes a little. "He has some very interesting results; however, I do not know what they are as no one has yet shared them with me."

"Oh!" said Kate, glad that all she had to do was take a little iron. Although the rationale sounded quite desperate, the cure—an iron solution—seemed innocent enough. Unlike the leeches, which she had better not have to endure again.

"Shall we see about my blue dress?" Kate asked as they went along. It was hard to keep track of it. It seemed that Doña Elvira was always sending it to be washed, and it was Kate's favorite—she wasn't sure why. "I mean, I imagine the laundry is done and we should go and collect the dress before it goes astray."

"Well, we could stop by the laundry on the way back ..." mused Doña Elvira. "Come along, then. We must make haste."

Doña Elvira led her down one corridor and then another, until at last they entered the doorway of a large, hot room.

Five men were at work over enormous pots of water boiling at four separate hearths. Doña Elvira asked about Kate's dress and was told that it was clean but not yet dry.

"We can just as well hang it in our rooms near a brazier rather than leave it here," Kate said.

"Well, all right," said her nurse. "But you will have to carry it. The damp cloth might bother my joints."

They passed one of the great kitchens on their way back to their quarters, and Kate couldn't help peeking in and commenting at the noise, the general flurry, and the state of the workers. Clothed in ill-fitting garments that were either too large or too small, and some, by the look of them, merely underwear, scullions were hurrying about from one pot to another, and Kate thought she detected sweat flying from some of their bodies into the broth.

"How awful!" she gagged. "I can't believe we eat this stuff!"

Doña Elvira grabbed Kate's arm and gave it a little shake.

"It's not for us to complain!" she said. "And it's certainly better since Thomas Wolsey gave the Clerk of the Kitchen money to purchase garments for the workers, even if the clothes are ill-fitting. There was a time when many worked without a stitch on their backs. I am also grateful that he passed a law about urinating on the cooking hearths, which was a nasty practice all around."

Kate gulped, trying to figure out how she could avoid eating anything that came from this horrible place. To see those kitchens, and to think about what might actually be in one's food, was disgusting. How she longed for the sterile cans of soup about which she had once complained. Then she shook her head at her own imagination. Cans of soup? What had gotten into her, thinking up such things!

It was hard for Kate to tear her eyes away from the kitchen. The cooks were putting tall glass jars into the cauldrons, each with different foodstuffs inside. One had chickens, another beans, while another had eggs. All of these jars could rest side by side within the same cauldron and cook the food separately, yet use the same energy.

Bright feathers caught her eye, and she turned to see a senior servant preparing a peacock for the table. He had fanned the beautiful tail up above the plate and was attaching other feathers into the breast. Better than a floral centerpiece, thought Kate, since the gardens were covered in November frost.

As Kate and Doña Elvira turned away from the kitchen, two scullery maids pushed past them without recognition.

"An' 'e gave us three candles," one was saying. "An' you know wot that means!"

"Wot?" the other asked. "Do you believe in that superstition?"

"Well, that I do," said the first. "There'll be a weddin' soon! Me own weddin', at that," she crowed, "thanks to those candles!"

"Of course," the other one jibed, "you don't know who you'll be marryin,' do you, now? Could be anyone!"

"Well, get on wi' you," said the first. "Wot person else would I be marryin' then! The Prince himself? I hear 'e's spoken for!" She howled with laughter. "Princess Katherine's wot you might call a lady in waitin'!" The girls scampered off, laughing, down the corridor.

"A lady in waiting," thought Kate. "Was that all she was?" *First comes love, then comes marriage, then comes baby in the baby carriage.* The bold children's rhyme, thrumming through her head, gave her an instant headache. If it were only that simple.

"Come on, then," urged Doña Elvira. "It's lunch time and I need a spot of soup."

Oh, no, not soup! thought Kate, agonizing at the idea of eating anything that had come out of those pots.

"I'm feeling a bit unwell," she said. "Perhaps I'll just go back and have a little rest."

When they entered their chambers, two servants watched with interest as Doña Elvira set the jar of leeches on the mantle. As soon as the nurse had left, Kate took one small step of independence. While the others were absorbed in their embroidery, she carried the glass jar into the garderobe and poured the creatures down the hole.

"Bon Voyage!" she whispered.

23
The sadness

By late November, Kate and William could see that the cub was growing quickly to adult size, and one morning at the farmyard, as they sat together in companionable silence, Kate wondered how long the creature could be kept captive in the coop. William was scratching the silky fur on the cub's belly and the animal was wriggling with pleasure. She admired his gentleness, grateful that he, too, took pleasure in quiet pastimes.

"I'm thinking we should find a way to set him free," she said.

"I'd rather be stuck in the mud and bowled with ... with onions than see harm come to him," said William. "But you are right. It's time, maybe past time. He's managed to catch rabbits and partridges, so in that way he'll be all right. But the hunters. We have to think of a way to protect him from the hunters."

"Maybe if he runs deep into the woods, far from here," said Kate. "Maybe then he will be safe?"

"Maybe," said William dubiously. She knew what he was thinking. It had become easy to guess his thoughts. MacQueen and the others rode on fine, fast steeds. They could cover a lot of ground.

"There's a price to pay for freedom," he said finally. "But no creature should be kept cooped up, away from the light of day, away from the things that give it joy."

"Yes," said Kate. "There is a price to pay for freedom." She knew all about it, for she had been paying it herself.

"*The Lord is my shepherd*," muttered William. "*He restoreth my soul: he leadeth me in the paths of righteousness for his name's sake ...*"

He stood up unsteadily and walked to the door of the chicken coop. Kate noticed how stooped he was and how, in the sunlight, his face was very pale.

"Are you feeling all right?" she asked, suddenly concerned.

"No," he said dully. "I'm not. But I'll ... I'm sure I'll be fine. I've gone at my studies a bit too hard of late. Perhaps I just need more rest. And I miss home. Mother makes the best butter dumplings. I wish you could taste them. Sticky on the outside, light and dry in the middle. She wrote me last week, asking about Father, and I haven't had the heart to answer."

"You're probably just homesick," said Kate, still conscious

of his white face. "It's hard, missing your family."

"Do you miss them, too?" William asked in a hollow voice, looking at her. "Your family?"

"I do," she faltered, a whole patchwork of images rising to attention. "More than I can say."

"It's more than homesickness," he went on. "It's heartsickness, too, thinking of Father in that terrible place."

"You're doing the best you can," said Kate.

"No," he said, "I'm not. I haven't been effective, you know, in engineering his release. I don't know if he can stand the rest of the winter in the Tower. It's damp and cold and the vermin are abominable. He won't be able to stand it." His voice broke. "I ... I won't be able to stand it."

"You're doing what you can," Kate repeated. She took a step toward him, then stopped at his expression.

"I'm not feeling well. It's all muddled up, you, and the Prince, and my father, and ... and everything." He leaned against the door frame and breathed heavily. "And someone keeps cooking onions somewhere. I can smell them."

"I'll walk you back," said Kate, flustered. "Maybe you just need a bit more rest, and by tomorrow—"

"No," William interrupted. "I'll go alone. There's talk, you know, of us spending time together. It wouldn't be good ... it wouldn't be good if this talk reached the King. He wouldn't want anything to come between ... between the match he is planning between you and the Prince." Delicately, William didn't look at her as he spoke.

He took a step out into the sunlight and staggered, almost falling. She ran to his side and took his arm.

"Today I'll walk you back," she said. "Another day we can worry about what the rest of them might think."

She left him at the door to the great hall where he said he'd take a little ale, and went back, worriedly, to her own chambers. He just needed some extra rest, as he had said, and tomorrow he'd be fine. But tomorrow he wasn't fine, nor was he fine the next day. It wasn't proper for her to enter his quarters so she had to rely on what she heard from Doña Elvira, who had various ways of getting information. On the third day, when she had made herself sick with worry, she enlisted Doña Elvira's help to go and see what was the matter. But it was too late. William Fitzroy was dead.

"It was the sickness," Doña Elvira informed her briskly. "Took him last night along with the newborn babe I delivered last week. It is not an epidemic but we'll watch to see whether more cases develop. You might need to stay a spell at Fulham if it looks like there's danger. And Henry, certainly, will be riding with the King should any other illness arise here."

Kate looked at her uncomprehendingly.

"He's dead?" she asked. "William is dead?"

Doña Elvira gave her a sharp look.

"Yes, and that's the end of it. Pay more attention to your

betrothed, my dear, and all will be well."

Kate went into her bedroom and sat down on the bed. So many people she cared about disappeared one way or another. She thought of Arthur and her mother. Then she thought about her father, her real father, whom she hadn't considered in a very long time. And Isobel. The sorrows of Kate's losses on top of Katherine's were truly too much to bear. And now William. It wasn't fair. It just wasn't fair! She couldn't ask about a funeral, for even if they had one here at court, she probably wouldn't be allowed to attend. But she wanted to go to him, to see him just one more time. How could someone so young, so full of dreams, so good, be suddenly taken? It wasn't just! She buried her head in her pillow and cried, and, once started, the tears wouldn't stop. What if everyone she cared about died?

"Katherine!" called Doña Elvira finally after an hour had passed. "Prince Henry has summoned you and you'd best get up and wash your face."

"I don't care," she muttered. "I'm not going to see him today."

"Katherine!" Doña Elvira came in and sat on the side of the bed. "I'm not sure what game you think you are playing, but your job is to make Henry happy. Your only job. His good friend has just died and he needs you now more than ever. Please, my dear, show some compassion and go to him."

Kate woodenly did as she was told and went out to meet

the Prince. Side by side, they silently walked through the castle gates and westward along the Thames. Kate could tell that William's death had touched Henry deeply.

At the water's edge, they saw oarsmen in their green Tudor livery, rowing Princess Mary in one of the state barges. Beyond that, they could see tall masted ships putting out to sea. An ache in Kate's throat prevented her from speaking and, finally, it was the Prince who broke the silence.

"My brother Arthur died when I was eleven," he said, "and then my mother when I was twelve. It sometimes feels as if people I get close to are only meant to leave me."

Kate looked at him and saw that his eyes were full of tears.

"And, of course, my little brother Edmund who died when I was nine. I used to carry him around in a sling. He was only a year old. He had the most cunning white-blond curls. I used to wind them around my finger. And then Edward, the baby who died with Mother. All around me, death. Death," he whispered.

There was nothing Kate could say. Her heart was suddenly cold. She understood his grief but she couldn't give him the comfort he wanted.

"My Father the King chooses that I should ride from here tomorrow," the Prince continued. "If others become sick, you shall go to Fulham, and Doña Elvira and your ladies shall accompany you."

Kate nodded.

"I loved him well, old William," the Prince said bitterly. "He was a good friend, a loyal companion. True until the last."

I loved him, too! Kate wanted to cry. What had begun as friendship had deepened, although she hadn't let herself pay attention. Now it was too late. William would never know how she felt. Hard as it was to lose him, she knew with certainty that it would have been better to realize her love while there was still time to share it. Not that she was free to make any choices regarding her life. The road ahead unfolded according to plan, and she shivered at the knowledge of what her life held. The hints Henry had given her about the Tower and what happened to people who crossed the Crown had not gone unnoticed. In fact, she had been dwelling on them often of late, as she had been dwelling on his quick temper and the unjust way he sometimes treated others.

An idea suddenly came to her that brought some comfort. She couldn't bring William back, just as she could not bring back her own father, but maybe she could intervene with the Prince about William's father. She swallowed hard and very carefully chose her words.

"I am aware that the one thing William wanted was to free his father," she began slowly, "who he was certain had committed no treason but was unjustly imprisoned. Do you think there's a chance of his father's release?"

The Prince looked at her in surprise.

"Well, it's just been a matter of time," he said. "My father the King now believes there was little wrongdoing and he has been waiting for the right moment to free the prisoner."

"I think the right moment is now," said Kate. "This is how you could show your love for William, if you gave his father the freedom he deserves!"

"Perhaps," said the Prince, touching a hand to his head as if in deep thought. "Perhaps some good could come out of this, if only the release of an old man who is sure to die within the year."

"Think of the blessing for his family," said Kate. "To have their father back at a time when they're grieving the loss of a son and brother. Oh, please, if you ever loved your friend, now is the time to show your great compassion and mercy!"

"By St. George! I did love him!" cried the Prince, and Kate saw that he was rising to the bait. "And I could see that the old man is released ..." He stepped toward her as if planning an embrace and then stepped back, but for a moment, she saw his eyes glitter as they had before in times of triumph. Everything in his life was a step toward mastery of things: a marriage to further cement England and Spain, a way to show his image as a strong and compassionate monarch. He didn't really care about her or William at all.

"It might be time to show our great power and compassion," Henry mused. "The people do appreciate sensitivity in the face of death."

Kate turned away from him. He was not the person with whom she wanted to spend her life. His temper, his ego, his willful nature were faults she had tried to ignore in light of the qualities that had made Katherine love him. Yet she, Kate, pitied him for his failings. How could he help but be anything except what he had been groomed to be—a willful and competent ruler? She pitied him with all her heart but did not love him. Powerless in the face of past, present, and future, she closed her eyes. What was there here for her? What kind of life could she expect?

"The people will appreciate our sensitivity to one of our dearest companions," Henry repeated, as if trying to convince himself. Kate steeled herself and when she spoke, her voice did not tremble.

"You are wise beyond your years," she said. "If he had voice to speak his thanks, your friend would be most grateful."

If William could have seen his father freed, he would have felt such joy. It was what he had set his heart on. A rush of pride carried Kate forward. She no longer felt small and insignificant. She had done something useful for someone else, at last. *The best any of us can wish for is to make good use of the time we have.* A tear spilled onto her cheek and she fervently brushed it off. *And to create joy for others.* It wasn't so hard after all. And for her, it wasn't the end. It was only the beginning. She thought of Willow and of Gran. As if pushing through the dark veil of Katherine's presence, Kate considered all she had left behind and knew it was time to go home. A current of determination ran through her veins.

"I shall not kiss you goodbye," the Prince went on. "In case any sickness should pass between us."

Kate nodded again, trying to keep her mind blank so that he could detect nothing from her tone.

"I feel quite well," she said, trying to sound light. "And I hope that this afternoon we might take the horses and go for a ride, to pass the time until evening when you must make your final preparations for leaving. A ride in the fresh air would be good for us both."

The Prince contemplated the idea.

"Yes," he said finally. "A ride this afternoon would be a fine idea. I will meet you at the stables after luncheon. The grooms will have the horses ready." He seemed to regain his composure and Kate thought he seemed older; she could detect lines around his mouth that signaled an accumulation of more years than he had known. Grief does that to a person, she thought, if you let it.

They returned to the palace and the Prince continued on to his chambers, but Kate turned back toward the old farmyard. It was now or never, she thought, shivering in the sharp wind that had stirred up out of nowhere to sprinkle thin flakes of snow. Kate picked up her pace. It was now or never.

24
Freedom

The young wolf, she saw when she opened the door of the shed, was excited, sensing something new on the breeze. Kate hurriedly led it outside and toward the open country. The fields stretched into woodland and the wolf sniffed at the scents that were wafting on the wind. Kate predicted that it would find rabbits somewhere nearby. Easy prey. She wondered if it would pick up the scent of man and recognize it as the danger it truly was.

Kate shut the door to the coop and when the wolf turned back, sensing a change in atmosphere, it discovered the obstacle. It looked at her for guidance and she beckoned toward the fields and forest.

"Go," she said. "It's time for you to go!"

Uncomprehending, it took a few steps toward her and then wheeled back toward the coop.

"Go, now!" she said, waving her arms. Then she turned

and started walking away. The wolf began to follow but she turned and sent a kick in its direction, an action whose novelty was startling but not fully effective. The wolf retreated for a few steps and then circled back. She turned and continued walking, and once again it followed.

"Get!" she cried, breaking into a run. Then she stopped and picked up a rock, throwing with surprisingly good aim. This time the wolf got the message and pelted through the tall grass toward the distant trees. As it ran, a bolt of energy thrummed through Kate as if she were picking up some frequency usually tuned to the wild things of the forest. She shivered as she reached her arms skyward, sending out words intended as a prayer, although she was unused to such offerings. With the open sky above and unexplored territory stretching ahead, she believed that anything was possible—for herself as well as the wolf. Sweet freedom beckoned! It was time.

Back in her own rooms, Kate excitedly put on the old blue dress and made sure she was wearing the jeans and shoes underneath. She didn't know if she needed these items, but it was better to be safe than sorry. If life were like algebra, you needed to add to one side of the equation exactly what you added to the other. She scratched absentmindedly at the rash that had developed on her back from the nights sleeping on dusty straw ticking and laid out her warm gloves and fur cloak.

There were small loaves of bread for lunch as well as rich turkey soup. Out of necessity, Kate had learned to eat without considering the cleanliness of the kitchen, but she dined in moderation, not wanting to take any more chances than she had to with the possibility of consuming human sweat. Every little while, Doña Elvira rang a dainty bell she kept at her elbow to chase away the large brown rats that edged closer to the table, discolored teeth protruding over their thin lips.

As they were leaving the hall, the Prince appeared and offered to walk Kate to the stables. Doña Elvira nodded approvingly. "Go, have a pleasant ride," she said.

The black stallion was glad to see the Prince, and joyfully nuzzled at his arm. Henry gave Kate an apple and she knew better than to take a bite. Instead, wondering when in history people had changed their minds about eating raw apples, she fed it to the horse, who whickered gratefully in return.

"We'll ride now," Henry decided, calling the grooms to ready both steeds. Playing right into my plan, Kate thought steadily.

"All right," she said. "Maybe we could see that deer you spoke of killing the other day. Is it hanging near the clearing where first we met? After I returned from Fulham Palace, I mean, some weeks ago?"

"The one from last day's hunt has not been hanging nearly long enough," said Henry. "But I don't doubt that poachers may have interfered with it. It would be wise to go and have a look. It is indeed in my favorite clearing."

Kate mounted Katherine's dappled pony and it tossed its head anxiously at her touch. Horses are smarter than people, Kate thought, realizing that the gray pony did not sense Katherine any more, now that she had made her final decision. She could feel Katherine's memories trying to thread their way back into favor but she brushed them away. No more dual personalities. It was just her, Kate, that she was fighting for.

The air was chill and mists rose from the ground like great ghosts, making Kate draw her cloak tighter around herself. As they rode along, she all at once thought she saw a shadowy shape slink through the trees, but although she turned quickly, she couldn't catch more than a glimpse of it. Was it the wolf cub? She hoped it would stay out of their way.

Kate didn't say anything to Henry about the wolf; in a flash, however, she knew he must have seen it, too, for as he reached down to grip his bow and quiver, his jaw was tightly clenched. Her heart leaped into her throat and she tried to call out with small talk.

"How big is the deer?" she asked and, after a moment, prattled on. "Was it quite easy to kill? What I mean is, did it put up a fight? You have hunted a lot of deer in these woods." She was saying anything that came into her head, trying desperately to distract him. "How many have you killed? A hundred? I would guess at least a hundred!"

Before long, they stopped at MacQueen's, the cottage a blurry shadow against a surprisingly white sky. Kate felt a shiver run down her spine when she saw the little man.

"There are still wolves in these woods!" Henry bellowed, and spat at MacQueen's feet. "Ride out with us and you will see, man!"

"I dunnae ken," whined MacQueen, shifting from foot to foot. "I was sure I'd had them all. But bad luck in these parts has brought back the creeshie bastards." He cast a bloodshot eye at Kate but said no more.

"Saddle up and ride," commanded the Prince. "And bring the hounds with you."

They wheeled around and headed back down the path, and soon MacQueen and six dogs caught up with them. He, too, had a bow and arrow, and Kate could see a knife holstered at his hip. This wasn't part of her plan at all. If she attempted to escape both riders, she'd be an easy mark.

It wasn't long until they found the deer, hung by its heels from the bare branch of a large oak. Its lifeless body gave Kate the chills, so similar was it to the first deer she had seen hanging there—the deer she had seen Henry kill in cold blood. She couldn't help but register discomfort at Henry's glee as he spied it hanging there. *That could be me,* she thought, *hung as a witch*! One of the ropes was loose, and Henry dismounted and stepped around the dead creature, talking quietly to himself as he admired its size, distracted for the moment from any thoughts of wolves.

Kate slipped down from the saddle, tripping in her skirts and falling into a great brown patch on the thick grass. Blood. She quickly got up and stumbled away from it, tearing off the heavy cloak.

While Henry was occupied with the ropes holding the deer, Kate looked desperately for any landmarks she might recognize. She strode further and further away from the animal, noting a marshy area that she thought she remembered seeing before. As she approached, the pungent smell of mint filled her nostrils. Yes, this was the place!

"Why have you taken off your cloak?" called Henry. "You cannot be too hot?"

"Yes, I'm very warm, actually," Kate called, and saw even at this distance a look of tension pass across his face.

"Perhaps you are not well?" he answered.

"Perhaps not," she responded. It would be good to keep him from getting too close.

Henry moved from one foot to the other, seeming to consider his options. Finally, when he spoke, his tone was serious.

"I cannot chance the sweating sickness," he exclaimed. "And so, after we are finished here, I will let MacQueen accompany you back while I ride on ahead. No air must pass between us."

Kate glanced at the little man who leered joylessly in her direction, rubbing his hands together. As he and Henry finished their work with the deer, Kate promised herself that she would never let herself be alone with MacQueen, not in a million years! She must escape and it was now or never!

She had only just hidden herself behind an oak when she heard Henry calling. After a moment or two, he gave a great cry and she saw him flash past on the stallion, his face a mask of fury. She automatically moved around the trunk so that she remained hidden to him, and then crouched down as MacQueen thundered by, yelling a number of words that Kate guessed were foul.

"Show yourself!" Kate heard Henry yelling urgently. "Show yourself." An arrow flew a few meters away from her, and then another, further from the mark. Blind shots, both of them, but still a stern and dangerous warning.

Suddenly she saw a streak of gray and, at the same time, heard Henry calling her name. Then MacQueen was calling, too, in his scratchy voice. She scrambled around the other side of the tree and then made a break across the clearing, the young wolf suddenly beside her, two desperate victims of the chase.

The wolf steered her through branches and brambles, and then Kate saw the shadow in the grass that signaled the tunnel's entrance, if you could really call it an entrance, filmy and luminous as it was. She made for it as fast as she could with the wolf pressing close at her side. She could feel its desperation, the thickness of its panic, and suddenly she knew what had carved the tunnel in the first place. She saw them in her mind's eye, a heaving mass of frenzied fur and flesh, driving themselves forward, away from MacQueen and into the future, clawing their way through the fabric that separated one world from another.

She didn't blame the wolves for tunneling to get out of this time. She herself would do anything to get away. She heard thundering hoofbeats and crackling brush in their wake and believed the riders were close—and she knew, to the center of her being, that this would be her last chance at escape. If she failed, determined as he was to get his own way, Henry would find a method to secure her forever in this place.

Kate stumbled, and at that moment the wolf cub turned back toward those who pursued them, screening Kate with its body. She took a step into the dim circle and as she did so, she heard the elastic thrum of an arrow and then a cry—a high, nocturnal scream of pain. Then she was whirled into motion, the breath locked in her chest, relieved that she was going home, but heavy with sadness at what she had left behind.

25
The future

Kate pushed her way out of the tunnel as the roaring grew louder, and then a sudden force flung her past the entrance, shapes and shadows racing along beside her, sand and grit stinging her face. She found herself on the ground, unsure if she were alive or dead, her senses dull. A pair of leather slippers lay nearby, and when she got up enough strength, she reached out to pull one toward herself. Familiar. Very familiar, she thought, and then lapsed into unconsciousness.

After what seemed like an eternity, she began to recover. Dazedly, she brushed at her eyes, trying to get her bearings. She was sitting on the grass. On the hill, she could see the Royal Observatory and, from here, she could also just make out the top of the Naval College. She remembered it now, remembered coming here with her class yesterday. Or was it today? She couldn't be sure. Had she been asleep? Had she been dreaming? If so, what a dream! She brushed at her forehead and something on one hand rubbed against her skin. It was a ring.

Kate's memory swung sharply into focus and she got unsteadily to her feet, staring down at the ring Henry had given her.

"How now, what have we here?" came a familiar voice, a voice that had for months been speaking inside Kate's head but was now somehow released.

Kate whirled around. The ground seemed to tilt under her feet with the weight of things. Princess Katherine stood before her.

"Are you ill?" cried the princess, reaching out her arms. "Is there anything I can do to help?"

"Yes," said Kate, regaining her balance. "I mean, no." She gingerly rubbed an ankle. "You and I have a lot to discuss."

"I must go back," said the princess. "I seem to have learned much and yet I have learned nothing. I do not know what sorcery has surrounded us but I want nothing more to do with it. Anon." She stepped into the tunnel.

"No!" Kate said, lurching toward her. "You mustn't go back there. It will end badly for you. Stay with me!"

"I will be a Queen and the mother of a Queen," called Katherine, her voice fading as if a great distance were already between them. "And that is all that matters."

"No!" cried Kate, the world shifting again until it was level, all things being equal, with Kate on one side of the axis and Katherine on the other. "Wait!" The tunnel began to slip and shimmer before her eyes, all at once extending into the distance like a gray asphalt highway, and then, in the next instant, turning upside down like another expanse of sky. She stood, uncertain of her place in the universe, until finally, stunned and bewildered, she found herself standing in front of what looked like a plain old animal's den. *Wolves,* she thought, turning as a sound in the underbrush caught her attention. Emerging from the bushes were two of them, one larger than the other. Mother and son. They stared at her with unwavering focus and then wheeled around and disappeared among the trees by the river. One, the smaller of the two, she recognized. The cub! It had made it through! Thank goodness, it's safe, she thought gratefully, although its flank dripped a thin ooze of blood. Nothing more serious than a scratch, thought Kate with relief. Then a more poignant thought surfaced. Who says families can't be reunited?

With a heaviness that anchored her heart as well as her body, Kate trudged along the path, numbly trying to retrace her steps. Soon she passed the *Cutty Sark,* the figurehead registering its old stern expression, and made her way across the wet grass, instinctively following a set of footprints until she found herself beside the Royal Naval College. On the ground lay her navy jacket. She picked it up with clumsy fingers and put it on, reaching into the pocket but coming out empty-handed. Her watch was missing.

It must be Friday, mused Kate—*Friday, October 13, the day of the school trip, or else how could I have stumbled back into my own tracks or found my jacket?* These thoughts were calm and logical, yet her mind was buzzing with questions. Had Katherine been in this time long enough to discover some of her own history? She seemed sure that she would be the mother of a Queen. How had she figured that out?

Kate knew that her class might be leaving the museum at any moment but she couldn't decide which direction to take. Two passers-by stared at her odd clothes and she slipped on the jacket, planning to make a run for it. She could offer some sort of explanation on Monday to her teacher. And the dress—no longer unfinished and covered in stains—she'd have to figure out something to tell Willow. Or maybe by leaving the flat unlocked tonight, that would offer the opportunity to say it had been stolen. *Stranger things have happened,* she thought.

She suddenly caught sight of the whole troop of them filing between the stone arches and hastily hid behind one of the outer walls of the museum. She'd stay out of their way until the coast was clear and then duck into the building. She'd just wait there until there was no chance of being seen. She wondered what would happen to her date with Hal if she lingered here for too long, and then, all at once, she realized she didn't care. Knowing what she knew about him, it was better to let that one go. History really can affect the present, she thought.

When she decided it was safe to do so, Kate slipped into the museum and strolled among the display cases. She dazedly looked at boats of different sizes and shapes, some on the ground, and some suspended from the ceiling, and then wandered upstairs, drawn by a crowd of people heading to the second floor. She was strolling along the exhibits when a glass shelf in the middle of the hall caught her eye. Trying to appear nonchalant, she headed over to examine its contents. What she saw there made her catch her breath. It was Henry's astrolabe.

A description underneath indicated that the astrolabe was from a special Tudor collection, on loan to the museum. It had been found at Henry's bedside on the day of his death.

Kate thought how the astrolabe had been one of Henry's most prized possessions, something he'd kept by his side as protection against his overpowering fear of dying. A flood of pity washed over her as she thought of him and of how he must have railed at the end in powerless desperation.

"Look, this here's from Henry VIII," called a portly middle-aged woman, stabbing at the glass with her umbrella and then turning to make sure her husband was listening. "He had a head for science, that one did. Always trying to invent gizmos of one sort or another."

"Right," grunted her husband. "They sell ice cream on this level. I'm just going to have a look."

"And this astrolabe was found by his bedside the day of his death!" shrieked the woman. "If that doesn't beat all! A big important king, quite big, from the paintings, and rather a nasty piece of work when all is said and done, and this is the thing he keeps near him at the last!"

Tears filled Kate's eyes. She brushed them away and turned from the case, unable to look any longer at the thing that Henry had prized so dearly. The thing she—or Katherine, it really didn't matter which of them—had given him. The thing that he trusted to chart his course. She hoped that in the end, it had guided him safely home, just as William's advice had guided her. *No matter how long it lasts ... the best any of us can wish for ... is to fill our place.* And Kate's place, she knew, was here with her family. For better or worse. Worse if you thought of Willow's soup. Better if you thought of how important it was to be with family. With whatever family you had. As soon as she got home, Kate was going to call Gran. There was so much she wanted to ask her.

Suddenly, the tall, lanky frame of Martin Brown appeared before her, his dark hair catching the light.

"Hello there," he said. "Are you enjoying a bit of history?"

"What?" she said, startled.

"Are you enjoying the museum?" he asked again.

"Oh. Yes. Yes, I am," she said, hearing an unfamiliar sound

in her voice and taking a deep breath. "History is more important than I used to think." As she spoke, the words came out eggshell smooth, still in the tone that surprised her. "I'm thinking ... I'm thinking about writing an article for the school paper. About wolves, actually." As soon as she said these words, the idea took hold. It would be a good topic for an article, and focus on conservation. After all, someone had to take a stand on behalf of the wolves. She'd check with Naomi to see whether the offer of joining the school paper still held. It would be good, Kate thought, to belong to something. And maybe Amandella could be persuaded, as well. That girl looked as if she needed a friend.

"We're just here doing a little exploring," Martin continued. "My brother's up for the weekend."

"Your brother?" asked Kate, staring at the tall young man who now stepped out from behind Martin.

"Will, this is Kate. Will's visiting me and my sister, Ellen, for a few days. He's from Dorset, where he lives with our parents."

"Will?" repeated Kate. "And Ellen is ... is your sister?"

Will smiled, his brown eyes steady, his expression pleasant, and reached out his hand.

"Pleased to meet you, Kate," he said.

"Oh!" she said. His voice. His height. His sandy hair. "You look ... you look like someone I used to know."

"I hope you liked him," Will said lightly as she took the

hand he was offering.

"I did," said Kate, swallowing hard. "I did, but it was—" she stopped, searching for the right words, "it was a ... a long time ago."

"What a smashing ring," said Will, looking at the pearl on her finger. "Is it a family heirloom?"

"It's from an ... an old friend," said Kate. "It's a complicated story. I'll have to tell you about it sometime." The realization suddenly hit her that Henry, grown from boy to man, had been gone for hundreds of years. You can't outrun death, thought Kate. Nor can you hide from it. It isn't something anybody can control. She took a deep breath. The only thing you can really control, she thought, is life.

"I think it's time I was getting home," she said.

"We're on our way back, if you want to come along in the car," said Martin. Kate nodded, realizing that Will had one leg in a cast and was walking a bit gingerly with a crutch.

"What happened to your leg?" she asked.

"Rugby," he said. "One of the reasons I've been off school this week. It doesn't hurt too much but it itches like the dickens."

Somehow I'm not surprised, thought Kate, the corners of her mouth twitching.

"Hasn't really slowed him down," said Martin. "But his teachers don't need to know that. A little time off school is often a good thing."

"Yes," said Kate, still in the strange new tone. "Yes, it is. As long as you keep learning on your own. The world has many marvels to discover." I sound ridiculous, she thought. As if I'm about five centuries old. This guy won't like me in a million years. But when she looked over at him, Will was smiling down at her, obviously interested.

They were heading toward the elevator and Kate felt the old panic thicken in her chest. She stopped and considered for a moment and then deliberately walked forward, entering the elevator as calmly as she could. Her fear of enclosed spaces was with her still, but it wasn't getting the best of her. She took a deep breath. *This is who I am,* she thought determinedly, holding the door open for the others. *This is who I am. And I can live with that.*

Author's Note

This novel borrows from the wealth history has to offer, while at the same time rendering a fictional landscape that fuels a narrative of love and death, learning, growth, loss and resilience. I am grateful for the help I have received attending to historical detail, while at the same time I am conscious that any errors are my own and not to be blamed on reviewers who offered me sage advice. At times I have consciously selected fantasy over fact, putting story ahead of authenticity, and for this I make no apology.

While some of the characters in this work are fictional, others are based on real people whose lives are further chronicled in historical texts. The prince who was to become Henry VIII was born June 28, 1491, and appointed Duke of York at the age of three. On the death of his father and just prior to his eighteenth birthday, Prince Henry became King of England in April 1509, and married his brother's widow, Katherine of Aragon, in June 1509, at Greenwich Palace.

Many sources describe the young man who was to become Henry VIII as handsome, charismatic, and charming, accomplished at music and sports, and with the reputation of a scholar. Yet by the time he died in 1547, he had the reputation of an abusive and domineering murderer, tainted in the death of at least two of his six wives.

In order to understand the man Henry became, it's important to acknowledge the pressures and allowances of the sixteenth century in Tudor England: in other words, Henry himself is not singly to blame for his future deeds. Rather, he was a man created out of a specific social setting, in a particular historical time, and had expectations heaped upon him due to his station in life as a child-heir to the throne after his elder brother's death. Although this understanding in no way excuses him for the ruthless decisions he made in later life, it does make his character more complex than that of a simple tyrant. Further factual information about Henry's life and times can be located in Alison Weir's non-fiction text *Henry VIII: The King and His Court.* Other useful sources of information about the context of this story include: Arthur F. Kinney and David W. Swan's *Tudor England: An Encyclopedia,* and Simon Thurley's *The Royal Palaces of Tudor England: Architecture and Court Life, 1460–1547.*

The character of William Fitzroy is loosely based on a combination of a number of members of the young Gentlemen of the Privy Chamber, including: William Fitzwilliam, Henry's Cupbearer, who had been brought up with the prince, and Prince Henry's cousin, Henry Courtenay, who was another favorite and whose mother was a relative of Elizabeth of York, the wife of Henry VII and Prince Henry's mother. Courtenay's father had been sent to the Tower by Henry VII on suspicion of treason and was not released until Henry VIII freed him when he became King. The idea of floating water meadows, attributed to William Fitzroy in this story, was actually devised by Rowland Vaughan and first practiced in Herefordshire. The psalm William quotes is actually from the King James Version of the Bible. William's statement, "I'd rather lie down in a ditch and be bowled with turnips," was inspired by William Shakespeare's lines given to Anne in the play *Merry Wives of Windsor*: "Alas, I had rather be set quick i' the earth / And bowl'd to death with turnips!"

An outbreak of the Sweating Sickness did occur in England in 1507; it was considered a different sort of illness from the plague, and, after a sudden onslaught of symptoms, including a sense of apprehension, cold shivers, giddiness, headache, and severe pains in the neck, shoulders, and limbs, a few hours later, patients might experience a sense of heat and sweating, headache and delirium, rapid pulse, and intense thirst. Patients commonly died within twenty-four hours, although sometimes, as in William Fitzroy's case, death was somewhat prolonged.

The persecution of people perceived as witches occurred in England since at least the early fourteenth century. The particular case of a "cunning woman" mentioned in the story is based on the following incidents: in 1583, the churchwardens of Thatcham in Berkshire sent for a cunning woman to find out who had stolen the church's communion cloth; in 1507, a girl run over by a cart in Cheapside, London, was reported as lifeless, but eventually she revived and said she'd seen Our Lady of Barking lifting up the cart to save her life.

Wolves also faced persecution in early Britain. Some reports suggest they were completely eradicated in England by 1500, while other research indicates that a scant number were discovered since that time. In the words of my character Martin Brown, "One can't be a hundred percent certain. Not a hundred percent certain. About anything, really." Thus, I have allowed that a few wolves were left in 1507, supporting this novel's environmental theme; it is possible that I am not completely historically correct in this rendering of the wolves' timeline.

The character of MacQueen is derived from a story indicating that the last wolf in Britain was killed in the Scottish highlands in 1743 by a well-known hunter of great renown named MacQueen.

William's story of Frank Hopkin, as told to Mary, was derived from a story about George Bucker in *Isoult Barry of Wynscote,* by Emily Sarah Holt, written in 1871. Holt's work was helpful in assisting me to develop William's storytelling voice, which I found to be the essence of his character. I was also playing on the idea that perhaps Holt's story of Tudor Times originated with William's storytelling, from a true story about Charlotte that was passed along until it reached the ears of Holt, who fictionalized it. Stranger things have happened in the world of storytelling.

Theophrasus Bombastus von Santorio is a character based on that of Paracelsus, an alchemist, physician, and astrologer working in the early part of the sixteenth century. Born Phillip von Hohenheim, he later took up the name Philippus Theophrastus Aureolus Bombastus von Hohenheim, and still later took the title Paracelsus, meaning "equal to or greater than Celsus." The first Paracelsus was a Roman encyclopedist from the first century known for his tract on medicine.

In terms of the setting, my choice to use the royal palace at Greenwich was based on the fact that Prince Henry was born there and spent a good deal of his youth within its bounds. Because there is little historical information available regarding the exact interiors of this palace, my research involved visiting Hampton Court, a favorite dwelling of Henry's when he was older, and basing Greenwich interiors on what I saw there. The Royal Naval College and Museum now stand on what was the site of the royal palace at Greenwich.

The *Cutty Sark*, a famous tea clipper ship first launched in 1869, was housed for many years in dry dock at the site of the former Greenwich Palace. The ship's figurehead was a witch, inspired by a character in a poem by Scottish poet Robbie Burns, and when I viewed it, I did think she changed expressions when I passed by ... or perhaps it was just a trick of the light. The *Cutty Sark* was severely damaged by fire in the spring of 2007. Vandalism was suspected.

In late autumn 1506, King Henry VII did send Katherine of Aragon and her household to Fulham Palace. There is some controversy as to why he did so—whether he was concerned about the developing relationship between Katherine and Henry, or whether he wanted to avoid having Katherine contract illness, or to retire in case she was already a carrier, historians continue to deliberate.

Many reports indicate that Anne Boleyn was indeed born in the summer of 1507 (although other reports differ, some pointing to the year 1501 as the time of her birth), and historical information also indicates that she did have a growth on her hand (some reports describe it as a sixth finger) which had to be removed. She became Henry's second wife in January 1533 (following an earlier secret ceremony) and Katherine of Aragon, who would not grant Henry a divorce, was told her marriage was annulled and that she was to move households. Katherine was banished from Henry's side and died in Kimbolton in 1536. The only surviving child of the match between Katherine and Henry was Mary, who reigned as Queen of England for a short five years (1553–1558), and was the first reigning queen since the disputed Mathilda in the twelfth century. Katherine thus became, as she had dearly hoped, the mother of a ruling female monarch.

Acknowledgements

I am grateful to the Mint Agency and all the folks at Red Deer for supporting this work. Thanks also to: Wilson for giving me Theophrastus Bombastus as well as the tachyon theory that inspired the time travel element of this novel within the context of real world physics; Connor for his close editing; Eric for his helpful suggestions; Sara Jayne Amundson, Erin Beresh, and Tally Derkachenko for their many good ideas and encouragement; Alison Weir for her suggestions related to part of an early draft; Sharon Wright for her answers to specific questions regarding historical detail; Yvonne Petry, a historian at the University of Regina, for her sage historical consulting work, and the University of Saskatchewan for support in the form of a research subvention grant; Rachna Gilmore for her clear vision and wise council; my cousin Beth for her stalwart promotion of my work; Elma Brenna for her warm encouragement; and my mom Myra Stilborn for her editing help. Appreciation to St. Peter's Abbey at Muenster for a peaceful retreat opportunity, gratitude to the Canada Council for financial assistance, gracias to my editor Peter Carver for the phenomenal literary partnership, and to my husband Dwayne, a big hug for his everlasting love and support.

Interview with Bev Brenna

For you, where did this story begin – what was the seed of the idea?

This book began with a short story manuscript written while I lived in England in the early 90s. I had been thinking about portals between worlds, and the picture of a girl on a swing, pumping higher and higher, jumping off, and then ... somehow disappearing ... was a strong image that kept coming back to me. Coincidentally, I had been reading about Henry VIII, and how charismatic he was as a young man.

Eventually, I decided that a time slip account of the relationship between a young woman and Prince Henry could offer a really good story, exploring how both parties in a relationship should respect each other and how "changing someone" is more difficult than one might at first imagine. The short story began with the girl disappearing in time, followed her developing relationship with Henry, and concluded with her coming back through the "swing" portal. In this version of the story, the protagonist imagined all to be a dream, but then discovered the pearl ring on her finger as a sign that what she experienced had been real.

Of course, there was too much action to make this tale work as short fiction, and because of the amount of work involved in writing a historical novel, I set it aside for ten years or so until I could attack it with the attention that it deserved.

Is this is your first venture into historical fiction? For you, what has been the most difficult aspect of writing in this genre?

I have a young adult short story, "Higher Ground," in a Ronsdale Press anthology titled *Winds Through Time*. The story fictionalizes events in the childhood of the suffragette we now know as Nellie McClung, a Canadian hero who championed women's rights. The research involved in writing that short story was exhausting, and I knew before going into the Henry project that it was going to take me a lot of time. Because of the incredible commitment involved in trying to "get the history right," I would suggest that historical fiction projects are for writers who truly like research. The research process is kind of like the plot line of Numeroff's picture book *If You Give a Mouse a Cookie*. Put one detail into a historical story and there's a whole sequence of things you have to do that connect to each other. For example, in the banquet scene, I had to think about what they'd be eating, and then how they'd be eating it, including what cutlery they'd use, and the serving techniques. That scene alone took a good deal of work.

In your story, you have used characters based on real historical figures. What is the challenge to a writer in using real people in a work of fiction?

Having the opportunity to read about real people adds richness beyond what the imagination can offer. Working with biography can be frustrating, however, because the demands of fiction pull the writer away from factual characters and events. Too many details can ruin the plot by weighing the story down. In a way, the relationship between fantasy and realistic fiction is like how we try to balance history with story line in the historical fiction equation. Both balancing acts require walking a tightrope between the real and the unreal, and doing all four at once in a historical fantasy (fantasy, realism, history, storyline) can be quite mind boggling!

Do you think combining contemporary times with a historical period through the use of the time shift device helps make history more accessible to young readers?
Absolutely. Realistic fiction is the most popular genre among children and young adults, because it elicits personal response. The challenge for historical writers is to make the story speak to readers with the same intimate feel—creating characters that demonstrate universal themes that transcend time and place. Maybe we're reading about someone who lived a long time ago, but in spite of the differences, the character's feelings and struggles are just like ours.

Historical fiction offers a means for readers to live vicariously in the past. In addition to reading for enjoyment, historical fiction offers perspectives on history that readers might not otherwise consider. Henry VIII, for example, has been villified in many non-fiction texts; yet it's important to realize that society shaped the man he became just as society continues to play a role in the people we see when we look in the mirror.

On one level this is the story of a disconsolate teenaged girl dealing with loneliness and a sense of being abandoned by the people she's loved. But you are also interested in another story: the treatment of wolves historically in England. What led you to weave this thread into Kate's story?

My interest in wolves began rather incidentally when I lived in London and realized the incredible history of these animals in the United Kingdom. As I searched for a way to develop a time slip portal that would work in my story, I suddenly saw the potential of the wolves as tunnel-makers, although I had to stretch their existence in England a little longer than historians might generally allow. Some sources suggest that the extinction of wolves in England took place before 1500; however, I hope that the small liberties I have taken in prolonging their existence will be excused.

As a young reader, what works of historical fiction were you most attracted by?

My grade 5 teacher, Mrs. Gaston, read us Marguerite de Jong's *House of Sixty Fathers.* Every day after lunch, the whole class would gather excitedly for the next chapter. I really did not discover other historical fiction works until a university professor, during my masters' degree course work, suggested I try Mary Luke's books, and I was completely enthralled. I suppose you could say that as a reader of historical fiction, I was rather a late bloomer. I hope I have made up for it since! Canadian historical fiction authors I'd recommend to children and young adults include the following: Barbara Haworth-Attard, Linda Holeman, Julie Johnston, Sharon McKay, Maxine Trottier, Ann Walsh, Irene Watts, John Wilson, and Paul Yee. Rachna Gilmore's book *That Boy Red* is terrific. I also recommend looking at the winners of the Geoffrey Bilson Award for Canadian historical fiction.

For a young writer interested in writing a story based in a particular historical period, what advice would you offer? The advice I'd give is the same for both adults and young people: read copiously in the field you are interested in writing about. Write as best you can a gripping story. Research (either before, after, or both before and after) the historical period you're focused on, so that you get the details as right as you can. In historical fiction, setting is particularly important as it is integral to the authenticity of the work. The actions, beliefs, and values of the characters must also be authentic to the time period. Then find an audience who'll give you good feedback on whether or not your work feels "true."